She put o... "I'm Lea...

Ben said the first words... something he never did. "You can't be!"

Leah grinned. "The last time I looked in the mirror, I was."

"But…" Words failed him. Again. This wasn't part of his plan. She wasn't part of his plan. Desperate times might call for desperate measures, but that didn't mean he had to hire a college student to be his daughter's nanny. Hadn't he told the agency representative what he wanted? *Sedate. Quiet. Dignified.* And didn't those qualifications translate into someone *elderly?*

"I'm sorry, Miss Paxson. Please come in." *So I can fire you.*

TINY BLESSINGS: Giving thanks for the neediest of God's children, and the families who take them in!

* * *

Books by Kathryn Springer

Love Inspired

Tested by Fire #266
Her Christmas Wish #324

KATHRYN SPRINGER

is a lifelong Wisconsin resident. Growing up in a "newspaper family," she spent long hours as a child plunking out stories on her mother's typewriter. She wrote her first "book" at the age of ten (which her mother still has!) and she hasn't stopped writing since then. Initially, her writing was a well-kept secret that only her family and a few close friends knew about. Now, with her second book in print, the secret is out. Kathryn began writing inspirational romance because it allows her to combine her faith in God with her love of a happy ending.

HER CHRISTMAS WISH

KATHRYN SPRINGER

Steeple
Hill®

Published by Steeple Hill Books™

Thanks to Kathryn Springer for her contribution to the TINY BLESSINGS miniseries.

STEEPLE HILL BOOKS

Steeple
Hill®

ISBN 0-373-87334-4

HER CHRISTMAS WISH

www.SteepleHill.com

Printed in U.S.A.

"For I know the plans I have for you," declares the Lord, "plans to prosper you and not to harm you, plans to give you hope and a future."

—*Jeremiah* 29:11

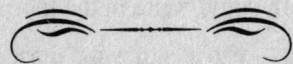

This book is for the two special guys in my life, whom God has blessed me with:

Reid—who spent a summer patiently emptying the dishwasher, answering the phone and waiting until after lunch to go fishing so Mom could write in the mornings.

And to Pete—who steadies me during the ups and downs of a writer's life and doesn't look at me like I'm crazy when I tell him there are people talking in my head (they're characters, honey, really!).

I love you both.

Chapter One

"**A**re you telling me there's a *nanny* shortage?"

Ben Cavanaugh tried to keep his voice even but he knew his frustration level had risen in direct proportion to the number of days he and Olivia had been forced to manage without Mrs. Baker.

"That's exactly what I'm telling you, Mr. Cavanaugh," Mrs. Wallace, the director of Tender Care Childcare, said seriously. "We placed most of our nannies months ago, when school recessed for the summer. I'm just not sure if we can help you. When did you say you needed someone?"

Yesterday. That's when he needed someone. Ben exhaled a silent, steady breath. If he were a praying man, this probably would have been the time to appeal to God to intervene somehow. He didn't. Instead, he reluctantly moved to Plan B.

"Can you recommend another agency?" he asked, pinning the telephone between his ear and shoulder as he searched his desk for a pen. The only one he could locate had a bright pink pom-pom where there should have been an eraser. He tested it on a piece of paper and the ink came out: pink glitter suspended in clear goo. He definitely had to have a talk with his daughter about what constituted a proper writing tool!

"If you can give me a few more days, I'm sure we can help you," Mrs. Wallace said.

Ben hesitated. Tender Care was his first choice. Not only did it have a wonderful reputation in Chestnut Grove, it was also the agency that had given them the woman Olivia had affectionately dubbed Nanny Baker—a soft-spoken, older woman who had lived with them the past seven years. Olivia had been three months old when Nanny Baker moved in with them and over the years they'd grown extremely close. He couldn't imagine another woman taking Nanny Baker's place in Olivia's life…or her heart.

But the reality was he didn't have a few days. "Mrs. Wallace, I appreciate it, but…"

A soft but audible click broke into their conversation. Ben knew what was coming next. He had call-waiting on his phone, too. "Will you please hold for a moment, Mr. Cavanaugh?"

"No problem." He leaned back in his chair and while he waited he studied a photo of Nanny Baker and Olivia that he'd taken during an outing in Winchester Park. Olivia had made the frame herself from craft sticks, glitter—lots of glitter—and an equally generous amount of glue. The two of them were smiling for the camera but for the first time Ben noticed that Nanny Baker looked, well, tired.

Reluctantly, he had to acknowledge the fact that with each passing year it had become more difficult for Nanny to keep up with an active child, no matter how good-natured. And Olivia was good-natured, there was no doubt about it, but her body was as busy as her mind, and her tongue had both of them beaten for speed!

When Nanny Baker had told him that her only sister in Arizona was recovering from surgery and had asked her to move in with her, he'd assumed that it would be a temporary arrangement. He'd immediately started compiling a list of *temporary* replacements until Nanny had gently corrected him. She'd been considering retirement for several months and was looking forward to being close to family again. Not, she'd quickly assured him, that he and Olivia weren't like family to her, but she knew this was something she needed to do.

Which was why they were now nannyless.

"Mr. Cavanaugh?" The director was back on the line, only now there was something new in her tone, a spark of excitement that hadn't been there before. "I was just on the telephone with Leah Paxson, one of our nannies. She was hired six months ago by a family in Richmond and she just found out the children's father has accepted a transfer to London that is effective immediately. She is returning to Chestnut Grove this afternoon and she, well, she's *available*, Mr. Cavanaugh. Isn't that wonderful news!"

Ben couldn't believe it. For a moment, he didn't know what to say. The thought chased through his mind that maybe God *had* intervened, but he shook it away. He knew better.

"Did you hear me, Mr. Cavanaugh? I can set up an interview between you and Miss Paxson tomorrow."

"She's well-qualified?" Desperate circumstances or not, he wasn't going to hire just anyone to look after Olivia. He owed it to both his daughter and to the memory of his wife, Julia, to make sure that Olivia had the best of care while he was at work.

"The family asked Leah to accompany them to London," the director said. "I know they've been extremely happy with her. She's worked with our agency for five years now and I've never heard any negative comments about her. She's a natural with children."

A natural. She certainly sounded qualified. Silently, he went through his schedule for the next day and made a few adjustments.

"How does eleven o'clock tomorrow morning sound?" he asked. "I'd like her to come right to the house. My office is here and I think it would be good for her to see where she'll be living if she accepts the position."

"I'll call Miss Paxson back right away, Mr. Cavanaugh. Eleven o'clock tomorrow."

Ben hung up the phone, relief pouring through him. Mrs. Baker hadn't wanted to go to Arizona until they'd found a replacement for her, but Ben had insisted, confident that it would be a day or two at the most until Tender Care provided another nanny. He hadn't considered that a week after her departure, he'd still be waiting. And now it looked as if the wait might finally be over.

Seven years ago, he'd told Mrs. Wallace exactly what qualifications were necessary for the woman who would be Olivia's nanny. Nanny Baker had fulfilled every one—quiet, sedate and grandmotherly. Ben could only assume that Leah Paxson would be just like her.

Leah Paxson was a firm believer in the adage, "When God closes a door, He opens a window." She reminded herself of that several times while pacing the length of her tiny studio apartment, praying about the interview that Mrs. Wallace had set up for her the following morning with Mr. Ben Cavanaugh. She was still a bit shell-shocked from the rapid change in her employment situation and although the family she'd been living with had practically begged her to go to England with them, Leah knew she had ties to the States that couldn't stretch that far.

She knew that God would direct her path, but she was still amazed at how quickly He'd answered! When she'd called Mrs. Wallace to explain what had happened, the director said she actually had a man on the other line who needed a nanny for his daughter. When she'd called back to set up the interview, all she'd told Leah was that Mr. Cavanaugh was a widower whose wife had died when his daughter was an infant. It would be a live-in position, of course, because he owned his own business and he was gone quite a bit. And the little girl—Olivia Cavanaugh—was seven.

Seven. Leah had felt a familiar but painful twist inside. Seven years ago, at the age of seventeen, Leah had given up her baby girl for adoption. After graduating from high school, she'd applied at Tender Care Childcare to be a nanny and discovered that caring for other people's children actually helped ease the ache in her heart, instead of magnifying it. With every smile or hug she gave, she secretly prayed that her own child was receiving one, too, from loving parents.

"You'll let me know, won't You, God, if You want me to take this position?" Leah asked, pausing in front of the window that overlooked the street. In the five years she'd worked for Tender Care, she'd always lived with the families who employed her but she still paid rent on the studio, needing the security of knowing she had a place of her own if necessary.

Flopping down on the futon that doubled as her bed, she closed her eyes, not accustomed to the silence. The family she'd just left had had three preschool aged children, which meant her evenings were filled with activity until the last one fell asleep. Usually by this time at night, she was tired, damp from being splashed with warm sudsy bath water and nursing a sore throat from having read Dr. Seuss at least five times. She didn't mind—it meant her arms were never empty, either.

Reaching out, Leah grabbed a pillow and hugged it against her middle. Her arms might not be empty now, but she could still feel an empty space in her heart. Maybe Olivia Cavanaugh would fill it, she thought drowsily as she fell asleep.

Ben glanced at his watch. It was only quarter to eleven. He breathed a sigh of relief. For a split second, he was afraid that the young woman, who was practically skipping up the sidewalk to his front door, was Leah Paxson. When he'd heard the slam of a car door, curiosity had drawn him to the window just in time to see a petite, slender woman slide from the driver's side of a VW New Beetle. A VW New Beetle the shade of a ripe honeydew melon. Its owner was just as unique. She was wearing a white lace shirt, khaki field pants that ended just below the knee…and something on her feet that looked suspiciously like combat boots. He couldn't quite make out her features until the breeze lifted her glossy brown hair and pushed it away from her face, revealing her profile. He frowned. There was something familiar about her.

He checked his planner again but there were no appointments until late afternoon. Maybe she was looking for Jonah. Jonah Fraser worked for him, and although he didn't seek female attention, it seemed to find him anyway. It gave Ben something to hassle him about.

The doorbell rang and Ben went to answer it, hoping that whatever business the young woman had with Jonah could be resolved in less than ten minutes. Before the new nanny arrived.

"Mr. Cavanaugh?"

Ben nodded. It was all he could manage. She was at least a foot shorter than he was and the eyes looking up into his were a warm, glowing topaz.

She put out her hand. "I'm Leah Paxson."

He said the first words that came into his head, something he never did. "You can't be!"

She grinned. "The last time I looked in the mirror, I was."

"But…" Words failed him. Again. This wasn't part of his plan. *She* wasn't part of his plan. Desperate times might call for desperate measures, but that didn't mean he had to hire a college student who looked like she was auditioning for a part on a teen TV show. Hadn't he told Mrs. Wallace what he wanted? *Sedate? Quiet? Dignified?* And didn't those qualifications translate into someone *elderly?*

"I'm sorry, Miss Paxson. Please come in." *So I can fire you.*

He pivoted sharply and heard her fall into step behind him. By the time they reached his office at the end of the hall, his frustration level had tripled. He was already behind on two jobs because of Nanny Baker's unexpected departure and now he was going to have to spend more time interviewing nannies. Even though Jonah had picked up the slack the past few days, Ben didn't like the feeling that he was neglecting his clients. And Tiffany, one of the teenagers in Reverend Fraser's youth group, hadn't minded watching Olivia in the evenings but she'd been hinting recently that the girls' basketball season would be starting soon.

"Sit down." He hadn't meant for his voice to sound so gruff but Leah Paxson didn't seem to notice. She was looking around his office with lively interest. In fact, she almost hummed with energy. It reminded him a little of Olivia. Silently, he groaned. Great, his potential nanny reminded him of a seven-year-old!

"You're a carpenter, aren't you, Mr. Cavanaugh?" she asked.

He nodded, not wanting to be drawn into pleasant small talk. Brutal honesty was necessary. "Miss Paxson, I have to tell you that I was expecting someone older…

much older. Mrs. Baker is in her sixties and she's brought a lot of stability to Olivia's—my daughter's—life. When I spoke with Mrs. Wallace on the phone yesterday, she didn't mention you were so young."

"I'm twenty-four," Leah said, giving him her full attention now. "I look younger because of my height, I suppose."

Twenty-four. Positively ancient, Ben thought wryly. He moved some papers on his desk and suddenly saw a bright pink sheet of paper that he hadn't noticed before, with Olivia's handwriting on it. The title read "Questions for the Nanny."

When had the little sprite put this on his desk?

He quickly scanned the list and an odd feeling began to sweep through him.

Are you frendly?
Do you read books?
Are you alergick to animals?
When you go to the park, do the swings make you sick?
Can you make macaroni and cheese not from a box?
Do you have rolerblads or can you borrow some?
Are you craby in the morning before you drink cofee?

As Ben read through the questions, he was struck by the enormity of their meaning. When he'd hired Nanny Baker, he'd deliberately chosen a woman who would be a surrogate grandmother, not a *mother.* To have hired someone close to Julia's age would have felt like a betrayal. But now he knew he'd missed something. Something important. Nanny Baker had been almost sixty when she moved in with them and already beginning to suffer from arthritis. She took Olivia to the park but sat on the bench and watched her while she played. And from the time Olivia could talk, she'd begged for a pet, but Nanny Baker was allergic to animals. Olivia had had to be content with a goldfish named Pearl. And he was pretty sure Nanny Baker had never discovered a passion for in-line skating!

He could feel Leah's gaze on him. "Ah, it seems my daughter decided to take part in the interview process."

Leah smiled and settled comfortably into the chair. "I'm ready."

There was no point. What he needed to do was tell Leah Paxson—politely—that he couldn't hire her, call Mrs. Wallace and ask her—politely—what in the world she'd been thinking, and start back at square one. His gaze drifted to the photo of Olivia and Nanny Baker again, then back to the young woman who sat across from him. She was too young. Too unconventional. Too…pretty. He ruthlessly squashed that wayward thought. But there was something about her…

"Why do I get the feeling, Miss Paxson, that if I tear up this piece of paper, somehow it's going to piece itself together again and you'll be back here tomorrow?"

"Mmm." Leah seemed to consider the notion and he caught a glimpse of a dimple in her left cheek as a slow smile drew up the corners of her lips and warmed her eyes. "Let me guess. You want someone firm, respectable and no-nonsense. Isn't that right, *Mr. Banks?*"

She'd seen *Mary Poppins,* too. And not just once, if she'd caught on that fast. It happened to be one of Olivia's favorite movies and he had half the lines memorized. And, thanks to a case of the chicken pox when Olivia was two, the lyrics of every song.

"Exactly so." His imitation of a British accent was so terrible he could tell Leah Paxson was trying not to laugh. He gave in with a sigh and looked down at Olivia's list. "Are you friendly?"

"I am friendly. But very strict," Leah said promptly.

"Really?" Somehow, he found that difficult to believe. Maybe it was the boots. "Read books?"

Leah nodded. "And play games...all sorts."

Ben felt his lips twitch. "Allergic to animals?"

"Not a bit."

"When you go to the park, do the swings make you sick?"

"The swings, no." Leah leaned forward. "But I hate the slide. I'm afraid of heights. Do you think that's going to count against me?"

"I think that evens it out. Can you, and I quote, 'make macaroni and cheese not from a box?'"

"Blindfolded with one hand tied behind my back."

Suddenly, he had a visual of Leah Paxson's face as she moved around the kitchen, with only her pert nose and softly curved mouth showing underneath a blindfold. His office felt warm and he cleared his throat. "Do you have Rollerblades or can you borrow some?"

"I'm willing to give it a try. But not without elbow and knee pads and a federally approved helmet."

Now he did smile.

"Crabby in the morning before you drink coffee?"

"I only drink herbal tea," Leah said, "unless someone happens to offer me a cappuccino with whipped cream and sprinkles. And I'm *never* crabby."

Somehow, Ben knew that the words he was about to say were going to change his peaceful, quiet home. Maybe forever. "Would you agree to a trial period, Miss Paxson?"

Chapter Two

When the door had opened, Leah was sure of two things. She was sure that Ben Cavanaugh was a man who didn't smile very often, and she was sure it would be divine intervention if she was offered the position.

She was right on both counts.

What she hadn't been prepared for was the fact that Ben Cavanaugh was going to be so—*just admit it, Leah*—so attractive. The fact that he'd been getting ready to terminate her, which at less than sixty seconds may have set a record for the shortest employment term in history, didn't lessen the impact his serious brown-eyed gaze had on her. Then, just when she knew she'd be back in Mrs. Wallace's office by noon, still jobless, he'd stumbled on the note from his daughter and his expression had softened.

Up to that point, she would have guessed he was a perfectionist who didn't allow room for error. The kind of man who made sure the people in his life had been carefully mitered to fit there. Then he'd totally blown her theory by showing an unexpected—and humorous—knowledge of *Mary Poppins*. Which just happened to be one of her favorite movies.

"Miss Paxson? Would a month's trial period be agreeable to you?" Ben prompted.

"That would be fine." She noticed that the humor had faded from his eyes. He already looked like he regretted his decision.

"Why don't you come by this evening to meet Olivia," Ben suggested, his tone once again distant and professional. "If you can start tomorrow, I'll arrange for your things to be moved over."

Leah thought of the meager possessions she had in her apartment. "Tender Care has always arranged those details for me," she told him, even as she silently admitted that it was her pride that didn't want him to know how little she actually owned.

She watched as Ben, still obviously lost in thought, picked up a photo on his desk, framed with painted craft sticks.

"Is that a picture of Olivia?" Leah leaned forward in anticipation as Ben handed her the photograph....

And felt like she'd been kicked in the stomach.

The little girl grinning at her from the photo looked achingly familiar. From the soft, wispy autumn curls to the wide, velvety brown eyes, the girl in the photo was a seven-year-old replica of Leah's mother, Sara Paxson, when she'd been a child.

"She's beautiful," Leah stammered, realizing that Ben was waiting for her to say something. "She looks like you."

It was only half-true. Olivia Cavanaugh may have inherited her father's coloring, but the heart-shaped face that gave her an almost pixieish look had come from someone else. Leah continued to stare at the photo, mesmerized.

"You aren't the first person to say that," Ben said slowly. "But my wife, Julia, and I adopted Olivia right after she was born."

Leah swallowed. Hard. It had to be a coincidence. A coincidence that Olivia Cavanaugh looked so much like the pictures taken of her mother when she was a little girl.

"We adopted her from Tiny Blessings Adoption Agency," Ben continued. "I'm sure you've heard of it."

Leah tried to maintain her composure even as an energy-draining numbness began to seep into every pore. Of course she'd heard of Tiny Blessings. When she'd gotten pregnant at sixteen, she'd made a sacrifice that had ripped out her heart, while at the same time it had given her child what *she'd* never had—two loving parents. And Tiny Blessings had placed her child with those loving parents.

Concentrate, Leah, she told herself. The photo started to get fuzzy and she blinked, focusing on the colorful plastic lei around Olivia's neck and the jeweled tiara on her head. "Was this taken at her birthday party?"

"Yes." Ben had a distracted, faraway look in his eyes. Leah could see the pain that shadowed them and somehow knew he was remembering his wife. "Olivia turned seven in May."

Now her mouth was completely dry. "May?"

He nodded. "May fifth."

Leah laced her fingers together to keep them from shaking. It didn't work. Fine tremors began to course through her body. She prayed that Ben wouldn't notice.

"I don't want to cut our interview short, Miss Paxson." Ben rose to his feet, signaling the fact that he was about to do just that. "When you come over tonight to meet Olivia, we can talk specifics about your job. That way there will be no surprises for either of us."

From his tone, it was obvious that he didn't like surprises. Leah rose to her feet, resisting the urge to wipe her damp hands on her cargo pants. "That will be fine."

"Miss Paxson?" Ben looked slightly uncomfortable.

Leah waited, her breath catching in her throat. Maybe he'd already changed his mind…

"Is what you're wearing, ah, the *standard issue* uniform for all the nannies at Tender Care?" He was staring down at her boots.

"Of course," Leah said, her sense of humor surfacing despite her agitation. It was one of the things that she'd learned over the years—to look for the joy in every situation. She deliberately widened her eyes. "You mean Mrs. Baker didn't wear hers?"

Ben stared at her. She knew he was intelligent, but somewhere along the way *his* sense of humor had definitely slipped its track.

"That was a joke, Mr. Cavanaugh."

"Oh." He forced a smile.

"This is my confidence outfit." He was still looking rather uncertain, so Leah realized she needed to explain. "Last summer I lived with a family whose oldest daughter was thirteen and very shy. I encouraged her to try out for a summer play at the high school and we went shopping before the tryouts for a confidence outfit. She let me pick it out. When the time came for me to leave and I had to interview with a new family, Christine took me shopping. Only that time, *she* picked out *my* confidence outfit. I promised her I'd wear it every time I had a new interview."

"So the boots…"

"You'll never see them again." The truth was she loved them. But if she had to choose between her favorite footwear and the chance to meet Olivia Cavanaugh, the boots would be banished to the back of the closet.

"Not that there's anything *wrong* with them," he said quickly. Too quickly.

"Is there anything else, Mr. Cavanaugh?" She really needed to find a quiet place to fall apart. At least she'd just discovered a hidden benefit of her boots—they prevented her ankles from shaking. "Did you want to check my umbrella to make sure there's not a talking parrot on the end of it?"

At the look on Ben Cavanaugh's face, Leah wished she had a rewind button on her lips. People told her she had a rather offbeat sense of humor and even though Ben had started the whole *Mary Poppins* thing to begin with…

"A joke, right, Miss Paxson?" he ventured quietly.

She nodded, not trusting herself to say another word.

"We'll see you tonight."

She ducked toward the door.

"Miss Paxson?"

Leah paused.

"Bring your umbrella."

* * *

Ben knew the exact moment when Leah's honey-dew-on-wheels pulled into the driveway. Olivia, who had had her face pressed to the window for almost an hour, gave an excited shriek.

"Daddy, she's here! Miss Paxson is here!"

He plucked the dishcloth off his shoulder, triple-folded it and hung it over the sink. "You can let her…"

The front door slammed.

"In."

He shook his head, realizing that his concern over Olivia accepting a new nanny had been wasted energy. From the time he'd picked her up from school she'd asked him a million questions about Leah. Then changed the order and asked them all again.

While he made supper, she'd taken it upon herself to dust Leah's room, even though no dust had dared to settle there while Nanny Baker occupied it. Olivia had even put some of her favorite stuffed animals on the bed as a welcoming committee.

He knew he should be relieved that Olivia wasn't grieving over Nanny Baker's departure but he still felt a bit uneasy. Especially since Leah Paxson was only with them on a trial basis.

He still thought she was too young. And too unconventional. And too…he clamped down hard on the next thought before it could surface again.

Nanny Baker had fit smoothly into their lives. The evenings in his home were generally quiet and orderly. By the time he got home from work, Olivia and Nanny had already eaten supper. Olivia had her bath while he watched the news or read the paper. Then, he helped Olivia with her homework. Nanny Baker read to her. He tucked her in. Together, they had been a well-oiled machine. Shortly after Olivia went to bed, Nanny Baker retired to her room, giving him the freedom to stretch out on the sofa with a bag of microwave popcorn and the latest bestselling suspense novel.

Why did he have the uneasy feeling that Leah was going to be the proverbial wrench in that well-oiled machine?

Ben exhaled slowly. More than anything, he wanted Olivia to be happy. In a sense, she'd lost two mothers. The first was her birth mother, who Ben had been told was a teenager when she'd had Olivia and given her up for adoption, and then Julia, who'd fallen in love with her on sight but had had only two precious months to hold her.

He tried to do the best he could, but many times he felt ill-equipped to handle the enormous responsibilities of being a parent, especially now that Olivia was getting older. With his mother living in Florida, he'd had to trust Mrs. Baker to provide a feminine influence in his daughter's life.

Now the question was, could he trust Leah Paxson?

Twice on the way to the Cavanaughs' home, Leah felt a wave of panic wash over her. When she was half a block away, she was tempted to call Mrs. Wallace and tell her she had decided to turn down the position.

She'd spent the afternoon sifting through the box of photos she'd inherited when her mother passed away,

trying to come to grips with the fact that Olivia Cavanaugh was the baby she'd given birth to. Seven years
ago. The child she never thought she'd see again. Not
only was her resemblance to Leah's mother uncanny,
but Leah could see Olivia in the pictures taken of *her*
as a child.

Now, as she turned the corner that took her into the
quiet neighborhood where the Cavanaughs lived, she
struggled with what to do. She knew Ben Cavanaugh
wouldn't hire her if he even *suspected* she was Olivia's
biological mother. He wouldn't understand her motive....

What is your motive? The question rose up and mocked
her, but it was her heart, not her head, that responded. She
wanted to know Olivia. And even though she had no in-
tention of hurting her, Ben Cavanaugh wouldn't care. His
first instinct would be to protect his child.

My child...

She whispered the words out loud and then, as the
house came into view, she saw a face in the living room
window. And then a blur of pink and lavender rushing
down the sidewalk toward her car.

God, help me. I don't think I can do this.

Immediately, the suffocating weight disappeared and
she was able to breathe again.

There was a light rap on the passenger window of her
car. Leah dared to look over and saw Olivia's smiling
face looking in at her. She slid out of the car and tested
her knees, wondering if they were going to do their job
and hold her upright.

"Your car is a funny color."

Now Olivia was right beside her, her eyes bright and

curious. Her finger traced a crooked path down the hood of the car.

Leah felt hot tears prickle her eyes as her heart struggled to absorb every detail about Olivia Cavanaugh. She was small for her age. Her hair had been expertly braided into matching pigtails. She was missing a front tooth. Her fingernails were coated with pink polish.

"Charlie is a little different." Leah forced herself to concentrate.

"Charlie?" Olivia's head tilted to one side, reminding Leah of a little bird.

"That's its name. And your name must be Olivia."

"Yup. But our car doesn't have a name." Olivia giggled.

As used to the sound of childish giggles as she was, this one went straight to her heart. Leah had expected Olivia to be shy, perhaps even resentful, of the woman taking Mrs. Baker's place. She hadn't expected the little girl to be so open and friendly.

When Olivia slipped her hand into Leah's, Leah caught her breath.

"My daddy told me all about you," Olivia chattered as they made their way up the sidewalk. She lowered her voice a little. "He said you don't like the slide."

"I think that for you I'd be willing to give it a try again," Leah said, allowing Olivia to tow her into the house.

"We can go down like a train," Olivia said. "Then you won't be scared."

Without warning, they turned a corner and Leah came face-to-face with Ben. He was standing in the kitchen beside the sink, obviously cleaning up from supper. Even dressed in work clothes, with his dark hair brushing the collar of his denim shirt, he looked like he'd just stepped out of a magazine cologne ad.

"Daddy, Miss Paxson said she'd go down the slide with me!"

Leah was glad that Olivia's presence deflected the attention away from her, because she wasn't sure she was good at pretending.

"Are you feeling all right, Miss Paxson?" He frowned at her.

Obviously she wasn't as good at pretending as she'd hoped!

"I'm fine." She forced her eyes to meet his.

He didn't look convinced.

Fortunately, Olivia was anxious to show her to her room and Leah was able to escape Ben's intense, brown-eyed gaze.

"Your room is next to mine," Olivia told her as they reached the top of the stairs and walked down the narrow hallway. "There's a door between them, but Nanny B didn't want me to use it unless it was an emergency."

"I see." Leah hid a smile.

"Do you think thunderstorms are emergencies?" Olivia slid an anxious look at her.

"Definitely."

"What about bad dreams?"

"Those, too."

Olivia's eyes reflected her relief. "Really?"

"And I think that cold toes and spelling tests and needing to talk are all emergencies, too."

"You do?" Olivia squeaked.

Leah resisted the urge to sweep the little girl into her

arms. Memories that she'd tucked away for seven years began to surface. The last time she'd held this child in her arms was hours after she'd given birth to her, when a sympathetic young nurse had brought her into Leah's room to say goodbye. Her baby's face was etched in her memory, the velvety skin of her cheek and the tuft of golden-brown hair on her head.

Olivia was patting her arm. "Do you like it?"

Leah snapped back to the present and realized Olivia was asking her about the room.

"It's perfect," Leah said, studying the small bedroom. There was a single bed positioned against one wall, made up with a pale green comforter and matching shams. At the foot of the bed was a beautiful trunk fitted with brass hinges. She wondered if Ben had made it. The floral curtains on the window were faded, but Leah thought they only added to the room's overall charm.

"This was Uncle Eli's room," Olivia said. "Daddy said the walls used to be brown." She made a face.

"Is Uncle Eli your father's brother?" Leah was anxious to piece together a picture of the Cavanaugh family.

"He's a doctor." Olivia bounced onto the bed, toppling a pyramid of stuffed animals that had been resting on the pillow. "He married Aunt Rachel. Aunt Rachel has pretty hair. She likes to braid mine." Olivia gave a long-suffering sigh. "I let her."

Leah chuckled. "I hope I get a chance to meet them."

"Aunt Rachel invited us over for Thanksgiving dinner," Olivia informed her. "Uncle Eli told me I'd have to help make the pies because Aunt Rachel only knows how to order them from the cate…" Olivia stumbled over the unfamiliar word.

"Caterer?" Leah guessed.

"Yup. And Grammy and Papa are coming from Florida to eat turkey with us. Papa always brings me a new shell for my collection."

Leah tamped down the butterflies that had taken flight in her stomach once again. In the past, the families she worked for had always given her holidays off. She'd never been included in the actual celebrations, and even though she and Ben hadn't worked out the specifics of her contract yet, she was sure that the Cavanaughs wouldn't be any different.

Olivia skipped across the room and opened a narrow door centered in the wall. "Do you want to see my room?"

"I'd love to."

Leah followed her into a little girl's wonderland. From the ruffled valances that framed the windows to the fluffy comforter on the bed, everything was iced in pink.

Over the past five years, Leah had learned to tell a lot about the children in her life by their bedrooms. With a quick glance around the room, she could see that Olivia loved books, stuffed animals and music.

She could also see that Olivia was well-loved but not overly indulged. There was no computer, expensive stereo or television in her room like there had been in some of the bedrooms of the children she'd cared for. Instead, there was an artist's easel, a bin overflowing with ink pads and rubber stamps and a microphone attached to a tiny boom box. On a nightstand next to bed, one lone goldfish with a filmy tail resided in a very clean bowl.

Her respect for Ben Cavanaugh rose even more. He was a good father.

Thank You, Lord. The simple words took wing from deep inside her. Ben Cavanaugh was exactly the kind of father she had prayed for for Olivia. The kind of father she hadn't had. And even though he seemed a bit rigid and controlled, she wondered if that hadn't come from losing his wife at such a young age.

For I know the plans I have for you. Plans to prosper you and not to harm you, plans to give you hope and a future.

The verse swept into her thoughts and Leah clung to it, just like she had the first time she'd heard it, shortly after she'd given her baby up for adoption. Her future had looked bleak. She was exhausted from carrying the guilt that weighted down her heart. But then she'd discovered that God loved her and had a plan for her. Those were the words that had brought healing to her life.

As sure as Leah was that God had brought peace into her life, she knew that He'd also brought her to the Cavanaughs.

Chapter Three

Ben paused in the doorway, realizing that Olivia was so caught up in giving Leah an item-by-item description of her favorite things that she hadn't noticed him yet.

It gave him a few seconds to study the new nanny.

As he watched, Leah put out her hand as if she was going to ruffle Olivia's hair, but at the last second she withdrew it and crossed her arms instead. He wondered if she was the type of person who wasn't comfortable with physical affection. When he was younger, he hadn't been much of what his mother liked to call a "hugger" either, but having Olivia had changed that. The first time she'd grabbed his finger and squeezed it in her tiny fist, she'd won him over completely to the hugging side of life.

For the second time that day, he had the feeling that he'd seen Leah somewhere before. Chestnut Grove wasn't that big…he must have caught a glimpse of her at the park or the diner at some point in time.

"This is Pearl…."

Olivia finally took a breath and Ben took advantage of the opportunity to break into their conversation.

"Is your room all right, Miss Paxson?"

Olivia let out a little shriek and Leah jumped. He was surprised her feet could leave the ground in those boots.

"Daddy, you scared us," Olivia scolded.

"I'm sorry." He said the words automatically, even as he noticed that Leah's cheeks were tinted pink.

"It's fine, Mr. Cavanaugh. Thank you."

"Miss Paxson said that I can use the door between our rooms," Olivia said. "But she has more emergencies than Nanny B had."

Ben tried to decipher those cryptic words and gave up. "I know you have a spelling test tomorrow, peanut, so why don't you study your list while Miss Paxson and I talk about some things."

Olivia looked disappointed but she nodded. "You'll be here tomorrow, won't you, Miss Paxson?"

Leah glanced at him, almost as if she were wondering if he'd changed his mind. Not that he hadn't spent most of the afternoon considering it! "I'll be here when you get home from school."

"Nanny B always picked me up," Olivia explained.

"Then I suppose I'll pick you up, too."

"Which is one of the things Miss Paxson and I need to talk about," Ben said meaningfully to his daughter.

"It was nice to meet you, Olivia," Leah whispered before following him downstairs.

Ben caught a whiff of something stirring the air that smelled like vanilla. He realized it was Leah. He quickened his pace a little and decided to talk to her in his office again instead of the living room.

"Olivia seems to like you." He motioned for Leah to sit down in the chair opposite his desk.

"She's a very sweet little girl."

Ben didn't like feeling off-center. And the truth was he'd been feeling off-centered since that morning, when he'd interviewed Leah for the job. "My work takes me away from home a lot, Miss Paxson, and even though Olivia is in school full-time during the day, I don't want her to be a latchkey kid when she comes home, making her own supper and waiting for me to come home in the evening. When Mrs. Baker left, I adjusted my schedule the best I could, but I will need you to take Olivia to school and pick her up at the end of day. I work most evenings until seven, and Saturday mornings, too. You can have one evening off per week and every Sunday."

He gave her a brief outline of the things that Mrs. Baker had taken care of and mentioned some of his own expectations about her duties. Finally he paused, waiting to see if Leah had any questions.

Nothing could have prepared him for the one she chose to ask.

"Where do you and Olivia worship on Sunday mornings?"

"Worship?"

"Do you have a church family?" She tried again.

"No."

A church family? What kind of question was that? But he knew exactly what kind of question it was. It was the kind of question that someone who was a Christian would ask.

He saw something in her eyes that looked almost like regret. But why would Leah Paxson regret the fact that he didn't go to church? *Maybe for the same reason his parents did.* The unwelcome thought pushed its way into his head. They'd always told him that when he lost Julia, he hadn't lost God, but he knew that was only partially true. How could you lose a God you weren't sure had been there to begin with?

Leah drew in a quick, unsteady breath. She could tell by the look on Ben's face that he didn't like her question. His expression wasn't the neutral one of someone who went about their day-to-day business and didn't think about God, either. He looked like someone who'd unexpectedly heard the name of a friend who'd betrayed him.

A red flag rose in her mind, but Leah knew she had a bad habit of turning red flags into banners. Yet she had an important question and she needed to know the answer.

"I go to Chestnut Grove Community Church," she said. "Do I have your permission to take Olivia if she wants to go with me?"

His eyes said no. His mouth even opened and started to form the word.

"If she wants to go with you." Those were the words she heard him say instead. And Leah could tell he was just as surprised as she was. "You've probably seen my brother and his wife there," he added tersely.

"Uncle Eli," Leah remembered, not able to place him by memory. There were two morning worship services so it wouldn't be unusual that she didn't know them. "And Aunt Rachel. Who uses a caterer."

She probably shouldn't have said that, but Ben smiled. "According to my brother, Rachel loves a challenge and she's decided that cooking is the newest hill to conquer. She insists on making Thanksgiving dinner this year."

"Olivia mentioned that. And your parents are visiting from Florida?"

"They'll be here the day before Thanksgiving. Do you have family in Chestnut Grove?"

The only family she had was studying her spelling words, but she couldn't tell him that. "No. My mom passed away three years ago." No point in mentioning her dad. He'd abandoned them when Leah was five and she didn't have a clue where he was.

"I'm sorry."

The two words were simple and Leah had heard them many times before, but she could hear the sincerity in his voice. He'd lost someone he'd loved, too. For a moment, Leah felt a brief connection with him. "Thank you."

Ben stood up. "Do you have any questions about your responsibilities or the schedule, Miss Paxson?"

The schedule. He'd gone over it at the beginning of their conversation, detail by minute detail. She didn't have any questions about it but she already had a few changes in mind!

"Miss Paxson…" Ben hesitated and Leah braced herself. She'd known him less than twenty-four hours and had already figured out that when he said her name and then searched for the right words, he wasn't going to be talking about an increase in her salary. "Mrs. Baker lived here for seven years. She became a member of the family. Like a grandmother."

Uh-oh.

"You may want to go out…or have friends over. Maybe even your boyfriend." Ben shoved his hands into his pockets. "I realize you have a life, Miss Paxson, and I know that taking care of my daughter is a job…"

The word *boyfriend* had temporarily frozen Leah in place, but when she realized what he was getting at, she knew she had to say something.

"Mr. Cavanaugh, this may sound silly, but taking care of children *is* my life. I'm committed to Olivia and it's not just because I'm under contract—"

"Technically, you aren't under contract yet," Ben reminded her. "Until the trial period is over."

Leah knew he hadn't meant to hurt her with his matter-of-fact words, but she couldn't imagine being with Olivia for a month and then leaving. Somehow, she knew a second goodbye would shatter her heart more than the first one. Getting to know her daughter, only to lose her again, would be even more devastating.

Ben plowed his fingers through his hair in a gesture that clearly communicated his discomfort. "While you're living here, treat this house as your home. I want you to feel comfortable here. That's all I meant. I wasn't questioning your dedication."

It was easy for Leah to see that she wasn't what he'd expected, but because of the circumstances, he'd had to hire her. He realized that she *wasn't* Nanny Baker, bless that woman's grandmotherly heart, and he was trying to create some order out of the chaos her sudden departure had created. The trapped look in his eyes told her he was navigating unfamiliar territory and Leah had a strong hunch it was something he didn't like to do.

She felt an overwhelming urge to see him smile again.

"Does that mean I can practice my cello?" She gave him a hopeful look.

"You don't really play the cello, do you?" He was beginning to catch on.

"No. The saxophone." She was rewarded by the glimmer of a smile in his eyes. Oh, well, it was a start. "I'll see you tomorrow, Mr. Cavanaugh."

It was getting late and even though her fingers itched to tuck Olivia in, she knew she had to be patient. *Tomorrow night,* she told herself as she followed Ben down the hall. Tomorrow she could put her daughter to bed and begin building bittersweet memories. He opened the front door for her and she suddenly remembered something.

"Oh, I forgot to give you this." Leah dug into her bag and pulled out an umbrella.

Ben's mouth slashed into a reluctant smile as he took it from her and held it up to the light, making a point to study it from every angle.

"Does it pass inspection?" Leah asked. "See, it's quite ordinary, just like me."

For a moment, she felt the full force of his gaze and there weren't any shadows lingering there. His eyes were warm and unguarded and his next words sucked the air out of her lungs. "I don't think *ordinary* is a word I'd use to describe you at all, Miss Paxson."

Chapter Four

"Looks like you have company."

Jonah Fraser's muffled voice reached Ben, where he was wedged between the wall and a built-in bookcase they were trying to remove with as little damage to it as possible.

"Man, that *can't* be your new nanny."

Ben closed his eyes briefly. Judging by the amazed tone in Jonah's voice, he suddenly knew exactly who the *company* was. It was anyone's guess, however, as to why they were here. Leah had been living with them for a week now and she still hadn't figured out the schedule. Either that, or—and his suspicions were growing stronger by the hour—she just didn't *care* about the schedule.

The first thing she'd done after she'd moved in was change suppertime. When he'd come home from work the day Leah moved in, expecting to eat a plate of leftovers at seven, he'd discovered the table set for three.

Olivia had cheerfully announced that she'd eaten a snack after school and from now they were all going to eat together.

The second thing was, she really *did* play the saxophone. And she played it from eight to eight-thirty every evening. Olivia claimed it helped her fall asleep but he found it difficult to concentrate on his novel with the mournful, steamy notes of a saxophone permeating the house.

Now it looked like he was about to discover yet another Leah-driven change. He slid out from behind the bookcase just in time to see Olivia and Leah walk into the room. Leah had a picnic basket tucked under one arm.

"We made you and Jonah a pie, Daddy," Olivia said excitedly.

Jonah swung Olivia up and perched her on his shoulder as she giggled helplessly. "This is a nice *surprise*." He grinned at Ben.

Ben glanced at Leah, who was carefully removing a pie from the basket. "Right. Surprise." He couldn't argue with that. Over the past week, his life had become one big surprise.

"We're making pies to take to Uncle Eli's," Olivia said. "Leah said it's always good to have extra to share."

"I'll go along with Leah," Jonah said in such a cheerful voice that Ben suddenly wanted to stuff *him* behind the bookcase. "I'm Jonah Fraser, by the way."

Leah straightened and extended her hand. "Reverend Fraser's son, right? It's nice to meet you. I'm Leah Paxson."

"Always labeled as the minister's kid," Jonah said, shaking his head in wonder. "You never outgrow it."

Leah smiled and Ben cleared his throat. One of Jonah's eyebrows lifted but Ben ignored him. Leah's amber gaze swung to him.

"I hope you don't mind that we stopped by," she said. "I told Olivia that when we finished making the pies, I'd take her to the Starlight for a hamburger and we decided we'd bring a treat over for the two of you on the way."

"'Cause I worked so hard," Olivia put in. "Two apple, one pumpkin and a cherry."

Jonah swung Olivia down from his shoulder and as soon as her feet touched the floor, she bounced over to her father. "We brought you apple."

Ben was still mulling over Leah's words. He didn't *know* if he minded that they were here. He remembered telling Leah where he kept a copy of his daily schedule in case she needed to get in touch with him. In an emergency. Maybe finding someone to eat an apple pie fresh from the oven was one of the emergencies on Leah's list. He sighed.

Olivia felt it. "Are you tired, Daddy?"

They were all looking at him now. He forced a smile. "Nothing that a piece of apple pie won't cure."

"So, you're risking—I mean eating—Thanksgiving dinner at Eli and Rachel's this year, hmm?" Jonah said.

The truth was, Ben hadn't even thought about Thanksgiving. He'd been too busy trying to finish his client's library before they returned from their cruise in the Bahamas. "At least we'll have pie." He winked at Olivia.

His daughter turned to Leah. "Maybe you can help Aunt Rachel with the turkey."

"Oh, sweetie…I won't be with you on Thanksgiving."

"Why not?" Olivia's voice echoed around the spacious room.

Ben saw a shadow pass across Leah's face, dimming the warm sparkle that he was used to seeing in her eyes. "Well, holidays are for families. I never spend holidays with the people I work for."

But she didn't have a family. Ben remembered her telling him that her mother had passed away. She hadn't mentioned a father and he assumed there must have been a reason why.

"But you're part of the family," Olivia insisted and then turned pleading eyes to him to say something.

He wasn't sure what to say. The bond that had quickly forged between Olivia and her new nanny concerned him. Leah was young and pretty, it was only a matter of time until she met someone and fell in love, got married and started a family of her own…and then she'd leave. Even though she was young, Leah was closer to a mother figure than Nanny Baker had been. Nanny B had loved Olivia but she had clear boundaries that defined her personal time and space. Since Leah had moved in with them, he hadn't noticed her creating any of those boundaries. She was available to Olivia 24/7. Even when she was supposed to take an evening off for herself, she'd taken Olivia to Chestnut Grove Community Church for a children's fun night instead.

Over the years, Mrs. Baker had taken the opportunity over the holidays to visit her own family, and as close as she and Olivia were, Olivia hadn't protested at all.

"Daddy?"

He'd hesitated too long. Leah looked uncomfortable, Jonah looked incredulous and Olivia looked crestfallen.

"Chestnut Community is hosting a community Thanksgiving dinner and service this year, Leah," Jonah interrupted cautiously.

Ben shot him an impatient look. For some reason, the thought of Leah spending the day elbow-to-elbow with strangers and eating sliced turkey off plastic plates didn't sit well with him.

"You're more than welcome to join us at Eli's," he said. "I know Rachel won't mind, and my parents will want to meet you."

As far as invitations went, it was everything that was polite and cordial, but Leah still felt as if a fissure had formed in her heart. It was obvious that Ben still didn't approve of her. But for Olivia…

She glanced down at the little girl. She'd missed seven years of holidays and now God was giving her a gift. The opportunity to spend one with her daughter. Even as she yearned to say yes to Ben's reluctant invitation, a niggling doubt settled in her heart.

What if Ben's family saw the resemblance between her and Olivia?

When she'd taken Olivia to children's night at the church on Wednesday, one of the women had assumed they were mother and daughter. Olivia had grinned widely at the mistake but Leah had felt a ripple of fear.

She didn't want anyone to put the idea in Ben's head that maybe she and Olivia were related.

People see what they want to see.

One of her mother's favorite sayings came back to her. No one knew anything about her past. They didn't know she'd given a baby up for adoption. She was simply the woman hired to take care of Olivia. That's what Ben's family would see when they looked at her. She took a deep breath.

"I'd love to spend Thanksgiving with you."

Before the words were even out of her mouth, Olivia's arms were around her waist.

Later that evening, Leah was doing a load of laundry when Ben was suddenly standing behind her.

"Are you finding your way around the house all right?" he asked.

Leah never failed to startle when Ben unexpectedly appeared. There was something about him that drained away her ability to think clearly. Or speak with any kind of intelligence whatsoever! At least it felt that way.

"You're a jumpy little thing, aren't you?" Ben frowned.

Only around you, Leah thought. The truth was, the sight of him did strange things to her heart rate. "If the floor creaked, you wouldn't be able to sneak up on me like this. That's what happens when you live with a carpenter, though. A squeak wouldn't dare take up residence in this house."

Ben leaned against the dryer and folded his arms across his chest, which stretched the fabric of his shirt taut across his torso. Leah felt like Alice in Wonderland—the laundry room was definitely getting smaller. She shifted her gaze to a point on the wall behind his shoulder, a safe focal point to dwell on instead of his lean, muscular frame and handsome face.

"I know Olivia put you in a tough spot today," he said after a moment. "Don't feel obligated to spend Thanksgiving with us if you have other plans."

The plans she'd had involved renting a video and curling up to watch it while eating a turkey sandwich. "I don't have other plans. If you're sure your brother and his wife won't mind me crashing their dinner party."

"What's that saying? The more the merrier? A Cavanaugh code, I'm afraid. My parents—especially my mother—live for family gatherings."

Family gatherings. Those two simple words squeezed Leah's heart. She knew some people took them for granted, but she knew she never would. If she were ever part of a family…

"Well," she said brightly, closing the top of the washer, "this is done. I guess I'll go upstairs now."

"No saxophone?" Ben's eyebrows shot up.

Leah's face warmed. "Making all those pies wore me out."

"Good night, Miss Paxson." Ben watched her scoot out of the room. She always moved quickly, but with an unmistakable grace. Like a dancer. He shook the thought away. He was almost finished reading his novel, but now he found himself wondering if he'd be able to concentrate on it without the mellow music of the saxophone playing in the background.

* * *

"I'll be right back."

Leah took a moment to slip out of the kitchen, where she'd been helping Rachel Cavanaugh and Ben's mother, Peggy, with Thanksgiving dinner. She retreated to Eli's study to stabilize her racing thoughts.

Lord, Peggy keeps staring at me when she thinks I'm not watching. Maybe spending Thanksgiving with them wasn't such a good idea.

Peggy and Tyrone Cavanaugh were openly friendly and welcoming, but from the moment Ben had introduced Leah to his parents, Peggy Cavanaugh had had a thoughtful look in her eyes. Especially when, in the process of telling Leah a secret, Olivia had pulled Leah's head down so they were cheek-to-cheek.

After that, Leah had offered to help Rachel in the kitchen, leaving Tyrone Cavanaugh to entertain Olivia with a new book about seashells that he'd brought her. But she still felt Peggy's gaze settle on her occasionally.

The chance to spend Thanksgiving with Olivia—and Ben—had been too tempting. Leah caught her lower lip in her teeth and wondered if she would make it through the rest of the day.

A chorus of groans suddenly erupted from the living room, where Ben and Eli were watching football. Leah couldn't prevent a smile. There was an obvious affection between the two brothers. She'd seen that right away.

Drawn to a framed portrait on the wall, Leah stepped closer and studied the Cavanaugh family. The picture must have been taken when Ben and Eli were in high school. Her gaze lingering on the two boys, she wondered who in the Cavanaugh family tree Eli favored. Where Peggy and Tyrone had passed on their dark good looks to Ben, Eli was blond with light green eyes.

"They were quite a pair. I credit every gray hair I have on my head to those boys. And I'm still getting them, so what does that tell you?"

Leah heard Peggy Cavanaugh's lilting voice behind her and her heart skipped a beat. Her plan to escape to a quiet place to think had backfired. Now she was alone with the woman who'd been responsible for her escape to begin with!

Peggy came to stand beside her. "Rachel and the turkey are in a standoff," she murmured. "But my guess is that Rachel is going to win the battle."

Leah would have to agree. With her chestnut hair and exotic hazel eyes, Rachel Cavanaugh could have easily been a contestant in a beauty pageant, but it was her easy confidence and warm friendliness that Leah had immediately been drawn to. That and the fact that the second the two women had met, Rachel had leaned over and whispered two words tersely in her ear. "Corn pudding?"

Leah could only assume she was being asked if she knew how to make it. She'd nodded. Rachel had discreetly looked at her watch and then flashed all five fingers at Leah. In that moment, any doubts Leah had had about her presence in Rachel's home were firmly put to rest.

"We adopted Eli when he was six years old," Peggy said softly. "His parents were killed in a car accident and Eli was with them but he only suffered minor injuries. Ben was seven at the time but we'd adopted him from

Tiny Blessings as a baby. We were never told much about his birth parents. Back then, the records were sealed, you know. Not like nowadays, when there are open adoptions and contact clauses."

Ben. Adopted. Leah felt her breath catch in her throat. She'd had no idea.

"It was good of you to give the boys a home."

Peggy shrugged. "I don't think goodness had a thing to do with it," she said honestly. "From the time I was a little girl, all I dreamed about was having a family. After Ty and I were married, we found out that I couldn't carry a baby to term. I had miscarriage after miscarriage. It was Ty who suggested we adopt. Funny how God's plans shape our dreams, isn't it? People tell me what a *blessing* Ty and I have been as adoptive parents, but the truth is, those two guys out there throwing pillows at the television screen are the blessings. All I know is somewhere out there, a young mother had a lot of love in her heart."

Since Eli's mother had died, Leah knew she was referring to Ben's birth mother. Or was she? There was a thread of *something* in the older woman's voice that made Leah uncomfortable.

Suddenly hungry to know more about Olivia, Leah dared to ask some of the questions she'd had since she'd moved in with Ben and Olivia. Questions she couldn't ask Ben. "Were Ben and his wife unable to have children, too?"

Peggy shook her head. "As far as I know, they hadn't been married long enough to start thinking about children. Julia was a nurse at the hospital and she was in the delivery room when Olivia was born. The couple who were supposed to adopt Olivia had just found out they were pregnant and didn't know if they could handle two children so close in age. They decided not to, but in the meantime Julia and Ben had prayed about it and knew they wanted her." Peggy's smile was soft. "It worked out the way it was meant to."

"You're doing great," the nurse told her. "It won't be long now."

"It hurts." Leah panted the words and felt the young woman's hand squeeze hers reassuringly, saw the compassion in her dark blue eyes.

"I'll stay here with you."

And she had stayed. Through the next two hours of labor and afterward. It was the blue-eyed nurse who had brought Leah's baby girl to her, wrapped in a soft pink blanket. So Leah could say goodbye. Then, she'd wrapped her arms around Leah when she'd started to cry.

The nurse had been Julia Cavanaugh.

Tears burned Leah's eyes. Tears she was unable to hide from Ben's mother. Her mouth fell open and her eyes widened. "I'm sorry, my dear. You must be a sensitive soul! I know I am. Ty teases me because I even cry during TV commercials."

Leah was rescued from a response by the pint-sized seven-year-old who suddenly careened around the corner.

"Aunt Rachel needs Leah," she said. "And Grammy, Daddy said to tell you he's got the chess board set up."

"That's my cue." Peggy brushed a stray curl off Olivia's cheek. "Every year your dad tries to beat me at chess."

"He said this is going to be the day he wins," Olivia whispered.

"He can try." Peggy gave them both a mischievous wink.

Leah stepped into the hall but was still having a difficult time breathing normally again. She felt a soft touch on her arm and forced a smile, assuming it was Olivia. It wasn't. It was Peggy.

"I'm really glad you're here, Leah."

Chapter Five

"You sit next to me and Leah, Daddy." Olivia dragged Ben over to the table, where a perfectly roasted turkey had taken its place as the centerpiece. Across the room, Rachel lifted her chin and gave him a smug look.

"How did you sneak all this food in, Eli?" he asked innocently. "Is there a chef hiding in the kitchen?"

His brother laughed and drew Rachel against him, planting a quick kiss on her cheek. "Don't worry, honey," he said in a stage whisper. "Next time we play football, I'll grind that attitude right out of him."

Watching them, Ben felt a pang of regret. He and Julia had only been married three years when the doctors discovered she had ovarian cancer. Although they'd known each other in high school, they hadn't started dating until she'd finished college and came back to Chestnut Grove. Everything in their relationship had been perfectly timed. He'd proposed after a year. They'd married eight months later. He thought he'd have a lifetime of memories with her, and now he found himself struggling to preserve the few but precious ones he had.

"Are you going to stare at that turkey all day or sit down and eat it, son?" Tyrone gave him an affectionate slap on the back as he headed toward the table.

Ben moved to take his place, which was between Leah and Olivia. Leah had a smudge of flour on her cheek and, without thinking he reached out and brushed his thumb against it.

She turned and their faces were inches apart. Once again he felt the fine jolt of electricity that had become annoyingly familiar whenever he was close enough to Leah to see the flecks of gold in her eyes.

"You had flour on your cheek." He showed her his thumb as proof.

"Oh." Leah's face was as pink as Olivia's bedspread. "Thank you."

Eli tapped his spoon against the rim of his glass. "Before we eat, I'd like to resurrect an old Cavanaugh family Thanksgiving tradition. Rachel and I thought Olivia might enjoy it."

Ben tensed. There was only one Cavanaugh Thanksgiving tradition that he remembered and both he and Eli had done away with it the minute they were out on their own….

"Under everyone's plate are corn kernels. The number you have is the number of things you thank God for during the blessing," Eli continued.

Olivia picked up her plate immediately and he could see the delighted expression on her face. Emotion shifted inside him. He recognized it for what it was—

guilt. He hadn't given his daughter any spiritual guidance over the past seven years. Hadn't taken her to church. Hadn't prayed with her the way his parents had prayed with him while he'd been growing up. Hadn't taught her to praise God for the blessings in her life or to lean on Him when things went wrong.

"How many did you get?" Olivia asked, craning her neck to look at his plate. "Daddy, you haven't even looked yet!"

He lifted his plate up and saw four kernels of corn. Four. If Eli had duplicated the tradition, the most a person got was four. Suspiciously, he wondered if some devious person had rigged his plate.

"I only got two," Olivia said, then leaned across his lap. "How many did you get, Leah?"

"Two."

Ben frowned. Leah's hand was clenched so tightly around the kernels of corn that her knuckles were white.

"Everyone ready?" Eli asked cheerfully. "Dad, why don't you start?"

Ben couldn't see a way to back out of this, so dutifully he closed his eyes. Four things he was thankful for. That shouldn't be so difficult. The hard part was *who* he was thanking. He liked to think that he'd worked hard to achieve the good things in his life.

Suddenly, he heard Leah's low, musical voice.

"Lord, I am thankful for Your faithfulness. And I'm thankful to You for bringing me to this table today, to share Thanksgiving with my—with the Cavanaughs."

"Lord," Olivia solemnly copied Leah's opening, "thank You for my dad. And for bringing Leah to our house."

Ben drew a deep breath and wondered why his insides suddenly felt as if he'd swallowed a box of rusty nails. Maybe because he hadn't talked to God since the day he'd shouted at Him…the day Julia had died.

"I'm thankful for my family and friends and my business. And especially for this seven-year-old stick of dynamite beside me." He heard Olivia giggle and his fingers found the ticklish spot on her knee under the table.

When he opened his eyes, he saw his mother squeeze Eli's hand and there were tears in her eyes. Ben knew why. At least one of her prodigals had returned home. But he wasn't a prodigal, was he? He hadn't gone out and squandered his life. Just the opposite. He'd done everything right. He'd done everything a Christian was supposed to do. He'd read his Bible and prayed. He'd been active in his church youth group as a teenager. He'd rarely missed a Sunday service. And Julia had still died. He'd realized seven years ago that he couldn't have faith in a God Who didn't fulfill His part of the bargain.

After the others had shared their thanks, and the dinner conversation turned to the upcoming Christmas holiday—another celebration that Ben had to grit his teeth and survive every year—Olivia suddenly bounced several times in her chair.

"I'm in a play at church," she said loudly.

Everyone fell silent.

"That's wonderful, sweetie," Peggy said with a quick glance at Tyrone.

"It's a musical. They picked parts last Wednesday when Leah took me to church. I'm an angel and I get to sing one song all by myself."

"And how did all this come about?" Ben asked quietly.

He couldn't believe Leah hadn't bothered to mention this to him. She'd obviously sensed his hesitation about Olivia going to church with her and yet she'd let her sign up to take part in the Christmas program?

"Reverend Fraser's wife, Naomi, heard Olivia singing with the group and she asked her if she wanted to be involved in the program this year," Leah explained, meeting his gaze directly. In the depths of her eyes, he could see a plea for him to understand.

And knowing how much Olivia loved to sing, he was supposed to be the pin that burst her bubble?

"From what I remember, Naomi does a wonderful job with the children," Peggy said. "Do you need a costume?"

"Leah is going to make me one," Olivia said. "It's going to have wings. And a halo. And glitter!"

Glitter. Of course it would have glitter. Ben struggled with his feelings. At his mother's encouragement, there were times when he'd volunteered his carpentry skills at Chestnut Grove Community Church, but he'd always managed to brush aside Reverend Fraser's gentle hints about attending services. Now, if Olivia was in the Christmas program, he'd be forced to spend Christmas Eve there.

There was an uncomfortable silence at the table and finally Tyrone's booming voice overrode it.

"Don't forget to give me and Grammy your Christmas wish list before we leave, peanut," he said. "We want to have time to find everything."

"There are only two things on my list this year, Papa," Olivia said.

"Only two?" Tyrone pretended to be shocked. "Well, that should be easy for an old grandpa like me to remember. What are they?"

"I want boots like Leah's."

Ben felt the turkey he'd just swallowed lodge in his throat. Boots like Leah's! But it was her next words that made him choke.

"And a mommy."

"Do you think Daddy's mad at me for singing in the Christmas program?" Olivia pulled the covers up to her chin so the only thing Leah could see was a pair of worried brown eyes. She sat down on the bed beside her. She knew that Ben was upset, but she wasn't sure what had triggered it—Olivia's announcement about the Christmas play or that a mommy was on her Christmas wish list. Maybe, Leah thought with a sigh, it was both.

"He's not mad at you, peaches." That much she was sure of. If anything, he was angry with *her* for not telling him about Olivia and the play sooner. Not that she could blame him. She'd been waiting for just the right moment, but the right moment hadn't presented itself.

There was a soft knock on the door before it opened.

"Ready for bed?"

"If I say no, can I stay up later?" Olivia sat up, her expression hopeful.

"It's already past your bedtime," Ben said. "Technically, you *have* stayed up later."

"I don't like *technically*," Olivia said with a deep sigh. She reached her arms up for a good-night hug.

Leah could smell Ben's clean, woodsy scent as he

leaned over and plucked Olivia right out of the bed, growling ferociously as he enveloped her in a bear hug. She shrieked with delight.

When the hug was over and Ben dropped Olivia back into bed, both of them were breathless and slightly rumpled. A swatch of Ben's sable hair had fallen over his eyes and his shirt had come untucked. Leah, who had watched their antics with fascination, was about to stand up when Olivia attacked. The weight of the little girl's impulsive ambush sent Leah tumbling off the side of the bed.

And right into Ben's arms.

She could feel the corded muscles in his arms as they automatically closed around her and they both landed in a heap on the floor. Olivia peered down at them, her eyes sparkling with mischief.

She picked up a pillow.

"Don't you…" Ben gasped.

Leah picked up the end of the sentence. "Dare!"

"Incoming!" Olivia sang out.

The pillow landed with a thump next to Leah.

"Thank goodness her aim is off," Ben murmured. His breath stirred her hair and Leah was suddenly aware of his steady heartbeat through the thin fabric of his shirt. Embarrassed, she rolled off him and jumped to her feet, not quite sure how she had ended up smack-dab in the middle of this unusual bedtime ritual.

"Good night, Livy." Now *she* was rumpled! Leah had braided her hair that morning and now she could feel loose strands escaping from all directions.

"Aren't you going to pray with me tonight, Leah?" Olivia asked.

It was something they'd been doing together for the past few nights. Shortly after Leah had moved in, Olivia had crept into her room and found her sitting on the bed, reading her Bible and praying. Olivia was so curious about praying that the next night, Leah had tucked her in and prayed out loud. A simple bedtime prayer, but Olivia had amazed her by joining in after she'd finished.

Leah felt, rather than saw, Ben's entire body tense. Now what? She was only in the Cavanaugh house on a trial basis. She was carefully marking off every day that brought her closer to that one month mark, when she knew she wouldn't have to say goodbye to Olivia. But she was already on dangerous ground because she'd taken Olivia to church….

Leah took a deep breath. "Of course I'll pray with you. Only you have to promise that you're not going to hurl any pillows at my head while my eyes are closed."

Olivia grinned. "I promise."

Ben started toward the door with a muttered goodnight and the smile faded from Olivia's face as the door closed behind him.

"Daddy doesn't pray."

Leah took her hand and squeezed it lightly. "Even if we don't say the words out loud, God hears them in our hearts."

Olivia's eyelids were heavy and she was practically asleep by the time Leah finished her prayer. She slipped quietly out of the room and went downstairs to put away some of the leftovers Rachel had sent home with them.

Ben was waiting for her, his expression unreadable. "I'd like to talk to you."

With a sinking heart, Leah followed him into the office.

Ben didn't bother sitting down behind his desk. Instead, he walked to the window and stared out into the darkness.

"I'm sorry I didn't tell you about the Christmas program right away," Leah finally ventured. "I should have."

He flicked a glance at her. "Yes, you should have."

Silence stretched between them and Leah moved to his side. She desperately wanted him to understand how important it was that Olivia be allowed to learn about God. Suddenly, something that Peggy Cavanaugh had said earlier that day came back to her.

"Your mother said that you and your wife prayed about whether you should adopt Olivia."

Ben's jaw tightened. "We did."

"Then you must know that God answers prayer."

"He does?" Ben turned toward her and she could see the hard glitter in his eyes. "Julia was twenty-six when she died. Twenty-six! I begged God not to take her and leave me alone."

Leah reacted instinctively to the raw pain in his eyes. She reached out and touched his arm. "He didn't," she said softly. "He gave you Olivia."

Chapter Six

Ben woke up the next morning to the smell of bacon frying. And the sound of giggling. He closed his eyes again. Olivia and Leah. Obviously, the two of them were taking advantage of the fact that there was no school and they were making a big breakfast.

Trying to tune out the sounds from the kitchen, Ben silently scrolled through his day. He didn't have to go to a job site, but he had a pile of paperwork and bills waiting for him on his desk. And he was pretty sure his parents would show up at some point to see Olivia before they went to visit his aunt and uncle in D.C. for a few days....

A mommy.

His schedule dissolved like sugar in water as Olivia's innocent words came back to mind. And had he imagined it, or had she looked at Leah when she'd so matter-of-factly announced item number two on her Christmas wish list? And who on earth had put that thought in her head in the first place? Ben stifled a groan into his pillow.

He hadn't dated since Julia died. He hadn't even considered it, even though well-meaning friends like Kelly Young had occasionally tried to set him up. His life revolved around Olivia and his business. In seven years there hadn't been a woman who had caught his eye or made his pulse kick up a notch.

"I want you to promise me something." Julia's eyes were full of love as she took his hand.

Somehow, he'd known what she was going to say. He opened his mouth to argue, but she'd put a finger to his lips. "Just listen to me, Ben. Someday, you're going to meet someone. Someone that God handpicked for you and Olivia…and I want your heart to be open. That's all I want you to promise—that you'll keep your heart open."

He'd promised, even though everything inside of him had resisted. He'd even worn his wedding ring until the day they would have celebrated their fifth wedding anniversary, when he put it away for Olivia as a keepsake. Between him and Nanny Baker, he'd convinced himself that Olivia had everything she needed. And now, out of the blue, Olivia had decided that she needed a mother.

There was a soft knock on the door and then Olivia poked her head in. "Me and Leah made pancakes."

He sat up and opened his arms, and Olivia dove into them. She was still wearing her pajamas but she had an apron double-tied around her waist. And she smelled like maple syrup and strawberry shampoo.

"I don't think I have enough willpower to pass up

pancakes," he murmured, planting a kiss on her cheek. "I'll be down in a few minutes."

She wriggled out of his embrace and skipped out of the room. It didn't take Ben long to shower and dress and make his way to the kitchen. The sight of Leah standing at the stove, wearing black sweatpants paired with an oversize white T-shirt and her hair still loose in a sleepy tangle around her shoulders, derailed any coherent thought.

His pulse kicked up a notch.

He remembered the warmth of her hand on his arm and the earnest look in her eyes when she'd reminded him that God hadn't left him alone.

If only it were true.

Leah glanced his way almost shyly. "Good morning."

Olivia gave him a gentle push toward the table. He sat down and waited as Olivia brought him a pancake so big that the edges drooped over the sides of the plate. It had blueberry eyes and a crooked chocolate chip smile.

He blinked. "Mmm. Interesting. Chocolate chips."

"That was Leah's idea."

Somehow, that didn't surprise him.

"Leah says that if you can't add chocolate chips to it, it isn't worth eating."

Ben raised an eyebrow. "Is that what Leah says?"

"I don't know that those were my *exact* words," Leah demured, the warm sparkle back in her eyes.

"So, what do you two have planned for today?"

"We've got play practice today," Olivia said. "And then Leah said we could rent a movie."

"I'll be working in my office," Ben told her, dabbing his finger on the end of her nose. "You know what that means."

"Do not disturb." Olivia's cheeks puffed with air and she looked disappointed. "Can you watch the movie with us?"

"Maybe tonight."

Leah put a plate of pancakes in front of Olivia that sent his daughter into a fit of laughter. "Look! Mine are caterpillars."

With chocolate chip eyes.

Ben shook his head. "Do you ever do anything *ordinary,* Miss Paxson?"

Leah tilted her head, sending a cloud of satiny, golden brown hair spilling over one shoulder. "These *are* ordinary, everyday pancakes."

In Leah's world, Ben realized they probably were. He found himself lingering over breakfast. Something he rarely did. Usually he ate a bowl of oatmeal, organized his schedule and was gone for most of the day. As he listened to Olivia chatter with Leah, he realized there were things about his daughter that he hadn't known.

She didn't like a boy named Austin Kramer, who pulled her hair during reading. She was self-conscious because her other front tooth was loose and she was sure that she was going to get teased when it fell out. And every day after school one of her classmate's parents brought their puppy along and Olivia always stopped to pet it.

Ben had a sudden epiphany. A puppy. Olivia had

wanted a dog since she was old enough to say the word. Maybe *a puppy* would push *a mommy* right off that Christmas wish list.

One could only hope.

"She has a beautiful voice," Naomi Fraser said as she slipped into the pew beside Leah.

"And quite a stage presence," Leah whispered back.

Naomi chuckled, unable to argue the point. Most of the children in the choir were standing stiffly, their faces frozen in concentration. Only Olivia was swaying to the music, her eyes bright and sparkling with life. While the rest of the cast was still using their printed scripts, Olivia already had her lines memorized.

"John and I are glad to see her here," Naomi said, referring to her husband, Reverend Fraser. "Even if Ben isn't able to bring her himself."

There was no censure in the older woman's voice, Leah noticed, only compassion. It made Leah respect her all the more.

"He wasn't happy with me for letting her sign up for the play," Leah said truthfully.

"But he's letting her take part in it anyway," Naomi said. "In spite of his feelings, he'll do what's best for Olivia. That's what loving parents do."

To Leah, Naomi's words were a balm to her soul.

That's what loving parents do.

She'd been sixteen years old and a high school sophomore when Jason Landes had noticed her. Wary at first, because Jason ran with the popular kids and Leah was more of a loner, he'd patiently worn her down over the summer. Hungry for attention and love and in spite of her misgivings, Leah had let her first crush develop into something more. Before Jason left for college that fall, he convinced her that taking their relationship to the next level would strengthen his feelings for her. Leah, already fearful that once he moved away he would forget all about her, was ready to do anything to secure his commitment.

A month later, she found out she was pregnant.

Jason's letters and phone calls had already begun to taper off, but Leah was sure he would be there for her when she told him. After all, he'd said he loved her. The minute he found out about her pregnancy, he'd accused her of cheating on him. He told her that he wasn't sure the baby was his, but even if it was, that she should "take care of it." He had plans for his future and he wasn't about to let a summer fling mess them up. When she refused, he hadn't contacted her again.

The pain of Jason's betrayal hadn't compared, though, to the decision that Leah had been forced to make. Seven months into her pregnancy, she'd gone to the Tiny Blessings Adoption Agency in Chestnut Grove. When she'd talked to a social worker and seen the pictures of the families on the wall, in her heart she knew she was doing what was best for her baby.

Naomi's hand squeezed hers. "I'm not telling you anything that you don't know, am I?"

Leah's throat swelled. What was Naomi saying? She searched the other woman's eyes but saw nothing in them except an offer of friendship. For a second, Leah was tempted to confide in her about the real relationship between her and Olivia, but fear of what would happen if Ben somehow found out kept her silent.

"How are you with a hammer and nails?" Naomi asked, rising to her feet.

"Clumsy," Leah said. "But willing."

"Follow me, then. We've got a stable to build."

On the way back from the home supply store, Ben saw Leah's car parked in the church parking lot. He glanced at his watch and saw that it was almost five. Banking his irritation, he changed directions and parked his truck next to hers. *Charlie.* He shook his head.

The minute he walked through the door, he heard a slightly off-key rendition of "Silent Night." And a lot of pounding.

Reverend Fraser came around the corner and saw him. He was covered in paint. "The youth group," he said by way of explanation. "They decided I made a better canvas than the backdrops for the play."

"I'm looking for Olivia."

"She's in the sanctuary having music practice and I believe Leah is working on the set in the basement."

For some reason, Ben found himself taking the stairs to the basement. He wondered briefly if Leah had become a walking piece of graffiti, too.

She wasn't. Perched on a ladder, she must have been safely out of the line of fire. Wearing a sweatshirt, and blue jeans so faded they were almost white, and with her hair pulled back by a colorful lime green bandanna, she didn't look anything like a nanny, but more like the teens also hard at work.

But then, the huge wooden structure she was hammering together didn't look like a stable, either, although he guessed that's what it was supposed to be. It was listing slightly to one side and totally out of proportion.

"Who designed the blueprints for this?"

"I don't think there are any." Leah muttered the words around the three nails pinched between her lips.

Ben raised an eyebrow and Leah's eyes widened.

"Was that a *joke,* Mr. Cavanaugh?"

"What can I say, you're a bad influence."

Leah pulled the nails out of her mouth and Ben noticed her fingers were plastered with Band-Aids. "So, what do you think so far?"

She looked so pleased with the stable that Ben hesitated to give his honest opinion.

"It's big." There. That was safe.

"We could always use a good carpenter."

Ben looked over the stable critically. No kidding. "I might have some time."

Leah started down the ladder, which wobbled precariously. Ben stepped forward and put one hand on the ladder to steady it and the other on Leah's elbow to guide her down safely.

She paused when she was two rungs from the floor and twisted around to face him. They were eye-to-eye. "Thanks."

"If you end up with that many Band-Aids hammering nails, I can only imagine the broken bones you'll end up with falling off a shaky ladder."

She jumped the rest of the way down. "Did you see Olivia yet?"

"I wanted to talk to you first. You said you aren't allergic to animals, but how do you feel about dogs?"

"I love dogs." She grinned. "Are you thinking about getting Olivia a puppy?"

"You're the one who's going to be stuck with it during the day so I figured I better talk to you first."

"I don't mind," Leah said. "I think it's a great idea."

"I found a few ads in the paper. If Olivia is willing, why don't we go check them out?" Ben had decided that the sooner he moved a puppy into the house, the sooner Olivia would forget about her Christmas wish.

An hour later, after they'd dropped off Leah's car at home and all clambered into his truck, Ben handed his daughter the classified section of the newspaper. "Can you tell me the addresses I have circled?"

Judging from Olivia's excitement when they'd told her the news, he'd made the right decision. She hadn't stopped bouncing since he'd said the word "puppy."

Leah was sitting in the back seat and he could hear them conferring in low voices. Suddenly, Olivia's pixie face was right next to his ear.

"How about this one, Daddy?"

He glanced down at the newspaper and saw one of the ads that the local animal shelter put in. Staring at him was a black-and-white picture of a dog. A dog of unknown origins with the name Bear typed neatly under his photo.

"Absolutely not."

"But he needs a home," Olivia said, panic in her eyes. "We *have* to adopt him, Daddy."

For three blocks, Olivia presented her arguments in a way that would have made a defense attorney proud.

He gave in. "I suppose we can look at the shelter."

If he was lucky, "Bear" would be gone.

The woman at the animal shelter was about to close up for the evening but took one look at Olivia's face and let them in.

"Do you still have Bear?" Olivia asked immediately.

No, no, no. The words pounded through Ben's mind.

"Bear?" The woman glanced at him doubtfully.

"From the paper." Olivia pulled the folded newspaper page out of her pocket and held it out.

"Yes." The word was drawn out slowly and the woman looked at him helplessly over Olivia's head.

Leah, who hadn't said a word on the way to the shelter, put her hand on Olivia's arm. "We'd like to see him," she said firmly.

Ben scowled at her. She smiled back at him. Cheeky nanny. As he stalked past her, he muttered two words.

"Trial period."

Leah coughed.

Bear was in a cage toward the back of the row of kennels. They passed at least seven dogs on the way to see Bear. Seven smaller dogs whose origins were more apparent.

One look at Bear, though, and he could tell the dog's origins. Large. The dog had feet the size of circular saw blades. His fur looked like a wire brush, a mixture of blacks, tans and grays with no pattern or specific markings.

"We are interested in a puppy." That should take care of it right there, Ben thought.

"Bear *is* a puppy. He's only six months old."

Six months old. Ben closed his eyes but when he opened them, Bear was still there. Only now he had sprung to his feet and was frantically trying to lick Olivia's face through the fence that separated them.

"I'd say German shepherd, collie and maybe husky," Leah whispered, a smile of pure delight on her face.

"Sure. The toy breeds." Ben rolled his eyes.

Leah laughed and it washed over him the way her saxophone music did. "I don't know…the shape of that head could mean a Newfoundland somewhere in the family tree."

"Or grizzly," he said under his breath.

"He likes me, Daddy." Olivia giggled and put her fingers through the wire to scratch the dog's ears.

"He's housebroken," the woman told them.

That was a plus. He pushed his hand through his hair, facing the truth that maybe this hadn't been one of his greatest ideas. All he could imagine was his leather chair chewed apart, plants tipped over and shoes punctured with holes.

The shelter worker knelt down next to Olivia. "I can show you some other puppies. We've got a really cute little cocker spaniel mix that just came in the other day. Bear is going to be pretty big, that's why no one has adopted him yet. Sometimes it's easier to adopt a younger puppy because it adapts to a new home more quickly."

"Don't you want to look at some of the puppies we saw in the other ads before you decide?" Ben interjected, hoping to add some additional weight to the woman's words. The puppy-finding mission wasn't going according to plan—it had begun to careen down its own reckless path. He'd assumed they would look at several litters, go home and talk it over and then pick up the puppy when it was ready to leave its mother.

"Everyone wants those puppies, Daddy. Bear might not get a family." Olivia turned her velvety brown eyes toward the woman. "I'm adopted, too. So is my dad."

Ben heard Leah catch her breath. He took one last look at Bear, who apparently knew a good thing when he saw it and whined softly.

"I guess we'll take him."

Chapter Seven

Leah braced herself as the shelter worker opened the door to Bear's cage. Instead of exploding out of his confinement like a furry missile, he merely stretched, lumbered out into the corridor and began to chew on Olivia's shoelaces.

"I'll just have your mom and dad sign some papers, then you can take him home with you," the woman said cheerfully.

Leah felt a moment of sheer panic. Ben shifted uncomfortably beside her.

"I'm the nanny," she blurted out.

The woman blinked. "I'm sorry. You both—"

"Is Bear up-to-date on his shots?" Leah asked before the woman could verbalize her next thought. The last thing she needed was someone commenting on how much she and Olivia looked alike!

"Yes, he is, and all our animals have been checked by a veterinarian."

Leah relaxed as the woman began a rambling commentary on how irresponsible some pet owners could be about neglecting their animals' vaccinations. Within fifteen minutes, Bear was officially adopted into the Cavanaugh family.

With Bear and Olivia squeezed into the narrow back seat of the truck, Leah was forced to sit in the front seat. Next to Ben. The interior of the vehicle even smelled like him. A subtle blend of soap and the woodsy cologne he wore. No match, however, for the blend of warm puppy breath and cedar chips that began to permeate the air.

Once again, Ben had surprised her. The second she saw Bear and the size of his paws, she guessed that Olivia was going to go home without him. Was it her imagination, or was Ben beginning to loosen up a bit? He was still way too serious, but lately she'd caught more glimpses of the dry sense of humor that lurked beneath the surface.

"Can Bear sleep with me?" Olivia wanted to know.

"I think we'll make a place for him in the laundry room," Leah said. "It's warm in there and the floor is tiled, just in case he has an accident or two while he's getting used to living with us."

Olivia accepted that and when they got back to the house, she spent the next hour giving Bear a tour of his new home. Watching them romp together in the backyard, Leah felt an arrow of sweet contentment pierce her heart.

Thank You, God, for bringing me here. For giving me the chance to get to know my daughter. I'd hoped that maybe someday, she'd find me…but I never imagined You'd bring us together so soon.

"Penny for your thoughts."

Once again, Ben startled her. Leah's hands began to tremble and she pushed them into the front pockets of her jeans.

"I was just thinking that it will be good for Olivia to have a playmate," she improvised, not able to share the prayer that had just spilled silently out of her heart.

A shadow crossed Ben's face. "Julia wanted a houseful of children. There was a verse in the Bible she liked to quote…something about a quiver."

"'Behold, children are a gift from the Lord. The fruit of the womb is a reward. Like arrows in the hands of a warrior, so are the children of one's youth. How blessed is the man whose quiver is full of them,'" Leah recited softly.

"I didn't realize I was living with a walking concordance," Ben said, but there was no humor in his eyes.

Leah knew that he still wasn't happy that she openly expressed her faith in his home. When she'd switched dinner to seven so that Olivia and her father could eat together, she'd added another change—they'd started to offer a prayer of thanks for the food. After having met Tyrone and Peggy Cavanaugh, Leah knew that prayer had been woven into the fabric of Ben's childhood and teenage years, but she also sensed that now he doubted whether God really heard the prayers of His people at all. Even something as simple as a mealtime prayer.

"It's too bad that some people don't see their children as a gift from God," he said, surprising her with his bitterness.

"Your parents do."

"My adoptive parents," he corrected her. "I can't exactly speak on behalf of my birth mother, can I?"

Leah struggled to find the right words. Would Olivia feel that way as she got older? "You think of Olivia as a gift, don't you?"

He flicked an impatient glance at her. "Of course I do."

"Then her…her mother's…decision was her gift to you. No matter what the circumstances surrounding a child's birth, that child is a blessing…a part of God's plan."

"I came to ask you if you'd like me to take you and Olivia out for supper tonight," Ben said, effectively closing down their conversation. "We've had a long day and with a puppy in the house, it's probably going to be a long night, too."

It sounded wonderful to Leah, who'd realized when they'd pulled into the driveway that she hadn't taken anything out of the freezer for supper. The play practice at church had lasted longer than she'd expected and then with their unexpected adventure at the animal shelter…

"My hero." She sighed dramatically.

Ben's lips twitched. "You're pretty easy to please, aren't you? Don't most damsels in distress want to be whisked away to a castle?"

"I'd be happy with a booth at the Starlight Diner and a huge piece of banana cream pie."

The minute they walked in, Ben noticed the covert but interested glances they received from the other diners. They took a corner booth and immediately a waitress brought them ice water and red vinyl menus.

Starlight Diner was definitely a step back in time. Decorated in the style of the 50s, it boasted an old-fashioned soda fountain, complete with vinyl stools. Booths hugged the outer walls, while black-topped Formica tables were casually scattered in the middle. Posters of Elvis, Marilyn Monroe and James Dean, among others, filled the walls.

"This is my favorite place." Olivia peeked out from behind her menu. "Do you think I can get a hot fudge sundae for dessert?"

"If you eat your dinner."

Leah and Ben said the words at the exact same time. There was a moment of silence and then Olivia clapped her hand over her mouth, but her laughter spilled through the seams in her fingers and rippled through the diner.

An elderly woman who was sitting at a table nearby leaned over. "My husband, the Lord bless his soul, and I used to do the same thing. After fifty-six years of marriage, we could almost read each other's minds."

A pensive look crossed Leah's face and Ben wondered what had caused it.

"There's no getting around a mommy and daddy who are on the same side," the woman admonished Olivia with a smile.

Olivia grinned widely and didn't correct her.

"People should take one look at you and realize that you're too young to be the mother of a seven-year-old," Ben muttered. He was surprised that people didn't realize she would have had to have given birth at sixteen or seventeen to be Olivia's mother.

Leah didn't respond. She was staring at the menu, the

faintest bloom of color in her cheeks. Ben expelled a quiet breath. Is this what he was going to have to contend with—everyone assuming they were a couple? Life was much simpler with Nanny Baker. The only relative people had mistaken *her* for was Olivia's grandmother.

"Are you ready to order?" The waitress, Miranda, returned to take their orders and Ben listened to Olivia chatter about Bear while they waited for their food.

"We should stop at the store on the way home and get him some more dog food," Ben said when he could get a word in. "I don't think that tiny bag the shelter provided is going to last him more than a day."

Olivia nodded enthusiastically. "And he needs some chew toys."

Ben thought about his leather recliner again and winced.

"I'll watch him during the day and do damage control," Leah said.

Somehow, she'd read his mind.

"You like Bear, don't you, Daddy?" Olivia looked concerned.

"I think we'll get along."

Satisfied, Olivia began to tell them about her play practice that afternoon. Leah was relieved that her chatter filled the pockets of silence that would have fallen between her and Ben. Ordinarily, she loved eating at the diner, but now she barely tasted the food that she'd ordered. The sick feeling in her stomach refused to go away. How many other people were going to comment on how much she and Olivia looked alike and how long would it take for Ben's suspicions to be aroused?

After they'd eaten, Miranda returned and said cheerfully, "How about dessert? It's on the house tonight."

"On the house?" Ben repeated the words in surprise.

"Compliments of Sandra."

Leah had noticed the owner of the Starlight come out of the kitchen several times during the course of their dinner. In keeping with the atmosphere at the Starlight, she always wore a frilly pink apron with an S embroidered on the shoulder. Leah had caught her looking their way occasionally and guessed that it was because of Olivia. The little girl had a way of lighting up a room.

"I believe you mentioned pie, Miss Paxson."

Leah's stomach pitched slightly but she knew it was an attack of nerves. At any moment, she expected the cook to come out of the kitchen and make a comment about how much she and Olivia looked alike.

Sandra Lange ventured out of the kitchen a few minutes later and Ben rose to his feet, waving her over. "Thank you for dessert, Miss Lange."

Sandra was so petite she had to tilt her head to look up at him. "I just wanted to…" She hesitated. "Please, don't mention it…Ben."

There was a curious inflection in her voice when she said his name and Leah studied her. Maybe it was the lighting, but it almost looked like Sandra's eyes had a glossy veneer of tears. Before she had time to wonder about the reason, Sandra had reached out to tuck one of Olivia's loose curls back into place and then hurried away.

By the time they got home, it was almost Olivia's bedtime. Ben took an exuberant Bear outside for a few minutes while Leah helped Olivia get ready for bed.

"Everyone thinks you're my mom."

Leah, who was pulling up the covers to tuck her in, froze. "I'm sorry." She didn't know what else to say. She could tell that it bothered Ben when people mistook them for a family.

"I don't mind," Olivia said, then lowered her voice. "I've been playing a game."

"A game?"

"That you're my pretend mommy."

Leah swallowed hard against the lump that suddenly lodged in her throat.

"Olivia—"

"That's all right, isn't it?"

"I…" Leah wasn't sure how to answer. What if she told Ben that she was pretty certain that Olivia was her biological child? Would he let her continue to live with them?

He doesn't know anything about you, a voice inside her argued. *He's going to wonder about the character of a girl who got pregnant in high school….*

The shame that she'd experienced years ago washed over her again.

You aren't that person anymore, Leah, she reminded herself. *When you asked Jesus into your heart, He made you new. You're forgiven.*

But even though she knew that God had forgiven her, she somehow knew that Ben wouldn't. Not yet. Like Olivia, it would be so easy to pretend that they were a family. Easy but dangerous. In some ways, it already felt as if she and Olivia had never been separated.

Olivia reached out and squeezed her hand. "I asked God to make you my mommy for real."

Now Leah's heart was completely shredded. "I can't be, Olivia."

"Why not? You live with us."

"You know that in order to be your real mommy, your daddy and I would have to get married."

"Okay."

"Olivia!" Laughter and tears waged war inside her.

There was a mischievous sparkle in Olivia's eyes. "Good night," she said innocently.

Leah wasn't fooled for a moment. "Livy…"

Olivia closed her eyes and a second later, began to snore very loudly and unconvincingly.

Leah gave up and rose to her feet. Ben was standing in the doorway. How long had he been there?

"Is she asleep?"

Another loud snore shook the lump under the covers.

Ben chuckled. "Well, I guess that answers my question. Bear is exploring the downstairs and somehow I get the feeling that he thinks sleep is a waste of time."

At one in the morning, Leah knew that Ben was right. She could hear Bear whining pitifully in the laundry room. Pulling her robe over her pajamas, she padded lightly down the stairs. She knew that Ben had misgivings about Bear and that he had to get up early for work in the morning. The last thing that would endear him to Olivia's new playmate would be a sleepless night caused by the puppy's lonely laundry room concert.

"Bear!" she scolded him softly.

He had heard her coming and was already waiting by

the gate, his tail thumping a cheerful beat against the ceramic tile. It was obvious he was awake and ready to play.

She unhooked the gate and caught him just as he was about to streak past her. "Whoa. You're not going exploring now."

Bear cast a disappointed look at her and nuzzled her hand. Sleepily, Leah decided to make herself a cup of tea and entertain him for a few minutes.

When Ben found them, Leah was curled up in his recliner with an afghan tucked around her feet while Bear lay at her feet, chewing happily on a knotted sock. *His* sock.

"You gave in."

Leah slid a guilty look at him. "I didn't want him to wake anyone up."

"Olivia can sleep through anything."

Bear lifted his head at the sound of Ben's voice and then trotted over to him, the sock swinging from the corner of his mouth.

"If you play with him, he's going to do the same thing tomorrow," Ben said with a sigh. "And then you discover you've created—"

"A monster." Leah bit her lower lip. "He'll get used to us and then he'll sleep all night."

"He'll get used to playing with you at…" Ben glanced at the clock on the wall. "Two in the morning." He tugged on the sock and Bear planted his furry back haunches on the carpet and pulled back. "I forgot what it feels like to get up in the night with a wide-awake baby. It reminds me of all the nights I was up with Olivia." He stifled a yawn.

Leah wasn't at all surprised to learn that Ben was the type of father who took an active role in every aspect of parenting. He could have made the excuse that he had to work early in the morning and let Mrs. Baker handle the nighttime routine, but he hadn't.

"Was she a good baby?" Leah asked casually, although she was hungry for every detail that would fill in the blank spaces of her daughter's life during the past seven years.

"She didn't sleep through the night for quite a while," Ben said. "I think she may have sensed the turmoil in the house when Julia got sick. A lot of times, I would take Olivia to the hospital, just so Julia could hold her. It seemed to calm them both."

Leah, whose mother had been chronically ill, was able to read between the lines and her heart ached for Ben. It must have been so difficult for him to become a father and lose his wife so suddenly. And then to turn his back on the only One who could truly comfort him…

"You've done a wonderful job raising Olivia," Leah said. "She's a happy, loving little girl. Julia would be proud of you."

Ben stretched out on the floor with the sofa behind his back and Bear took advantage of the situation to plan a sneak attack. "Every time Olivia would do something new her first year, all I could think of was that Julia was missing it. Her first belly laugh. The first time she rolled over in her crib. The day she took her first step."

"You miss her."

Ben's eyes were haunted. "That's the worst part. We were married for such a brief time that I think what I miss the most is all the things we dreamed about doing and never got the chance to. When the doctors found the cancer, they scheduled surgery right away. They told me that she was young, that she'd be able to beat it. None of us expected that she'd develop a blood clot afterward and that within minutes she'd be gone."

Ben hadn't talked about Julia for a long time. Every time he did, the memories opened an empty cavern inside of him that took days to close again. He knew people had assumed he'd come out of his grief, but the truth was, it had become a tight knot inside of him that he didn't know what to do with. His parents had urged him to "give it to the Lord" but Ben resisted that. To his way of thinking, God could have healed Julia. How could he turn his grief over to God when He was the one who'd caused it to begin with?

Chapter Eight

Leah was amazed when Ben showed up at the church the following afternoon, wearing his tool belt. Amazed... and pleased.

After opening up about Julia the night before, he'd left the room abruptly with a muttered good-night. She knew how much strength it took to carry the weight of the past. She'd tried it herself for a while, until she'd realized that God wanted her to shift her burdens over to Him. It was something that Ben had to realize on his own, but still she added her prayers to the ones she knew were already being said by Ben's family on his behalf.

Olivia had another practice for the Christmas program and while she had gathered with the rest of the children upstairs in the sanctuary, Leah had been in the basement for the past hour, sanding the edges of the wood so that none of their pint-sized shepherds would end up with splinters. The kids in Reverend Fraser's youth group had been helping, but in the last thirty minutes, their numbers had dwindled as they'd gone on a church-wide search for snacks.

"How does it look?"

Ben studied it. "Like a huge bird feeder?"

Leah hid a grin. "I should know better than to ask a carpenter who probably sleeps with a tape measure under his pillow."

"I just figured with the play less than a month away, you could use all the help you could get."

"And you'd be right about that." Leah caught a glimpse of furtive movement behind Ben. Then a war-cry split the air…and before Leah could warn him, he was suddenly being attacked by kids armed with paintbrushes.

"Hey!"

The sound of Ben's voice froze them in place.

"I'm sorry…we thought you were Jonah," one of the girls stammered.

Leah pressed her lips together to keep from smiling at the sight of Ben's makeover. He looked like a rainbow.

"Jonah?" Ben repeated the name in disbelief.

"You look kind of like him from the back," one of the boys said defensively. As if it was Ben's fault that he looked like Jonah from the back!

Dylan. Leah had only been around him a few times but instinctively she knew that his tough guy facade was just that…a facade. From conversations she'd had with Anne Smith while they worked together at the church nursery, she'd learned that Caleb had made a lot of progress with Dylan, but the boy still had a difficult time trusting people.

She slid a glance at Ben. Judging by the look on Ben's face, his sense of humor—the one she knew he had—was temporarily out of order. She sprinted over to a coffee can sitting next to the Bethlehem star and grabbed two paint brushes out of it. She slipped one in Ben's hand. It dripped red paint on his shoe. Oops.

"There are ways to make them pay for what they've done," she whispered in a thick accent, using her brush to cut a Z in the air.

"Leah, I don't think—"

"Yes, you do. Way too much sometimes," Leah said with a grin. "But this isn't the time to think, this is the time to *act!*"

She sprang forward and painted a broad red stripe right down the front of Dylan's shirt. He yelped in surprise but then retaliated.

Leah was suddenly surrounded, but then Ben joined the fray. Within minutes, they all looked like rainbows until Caleb Williams, the youth pastor, poked his head in the doorway.

"Hey guys, I ordered some pizzas." He took in the scene before him without a blink. "Okay, who do I have to thank for this fiasco?" Without waiting for an answer, he pointed down the hall. "Get cleaned up. Don't track paint on the floor and meet back at the kitchen in ten minutes."

As the kids shuffled past him, he looked at Leah and Ben. "That goes for you two." Laughing, he shook his head and followed "his kids" out the door.

"Hold still. You have a glob of yellow paint by your ear. If that gets inside, you'll never be able to hear again."

Leah held her breath as Ben's hand touched her hair. He was close enough that she could feel the warmth of his body.

"Is it gone?"

"The yellow is, but I just added green and red," Ben said wryly. "I didn't know coming to church was so dangerous."

"Daddy!" Olivia rushed in with two of her friends and burst out laughing when she saw them. "Mrs. Fraser said you were here. We're going to go practice our play on the stage in a few minutes. Will you come and watch? I'm going to say my lines."

Ben hesitated. "Sure, sweetheart."

Olivia's face lit up. "Hurry!"

"We'll be there as soon as we clean up," Leah told her.

"Which should only take a day or two," Ben said under his breath.

Olivia nodded. As if on silent cue, the three little girls clasped hands, linking them together like a strand of pearls, and then dashed away.

"Sorry I didn't get a chance to help you with the set," Ben said.

Leah brushed away his comment with a smile. "Are you kidding? Do you think I could have fended off that attack by myself?"

"Without a doubt."

Leah's pulse settled back into its normal rhythm now that Ben had moved away. What was happening to her?

Something was wrong with Olivia. Ben stood next to Leah as the children lined up in the front of the church to practice, but something had snuffed out the light in her eyes. She shuffled from foot to foot almost nervously and she wouldn't meet his eyes.

He wondered if Leah had noticed.

Naomi Fraser shepherded a wiggling group of three-year-olds into a spot near the piano and then motioned to one of the parents to dim the lights.

"Can I have a script, Mrs. Fraser?" Ben heard Olivia ask.

Even from the distance that separated them, he could see Naomi's look of surprise. "You know your lines by heart, Olivia. Why don't you try it without the script?"

Olivia nodded and moved back to her spot, but he could still see the dejected slope of her shoulders.

"What's the matter?" Leah murmured.

"I don't know." Ben frowned. "Five minutes ago everything was fine."

When the time came for Olivia to say her lines, she looked down at the floor and remained silent. Naomi prompted her gently and finally Olivia stammered through them, nothing at all like the confident little girl he was used to. After practice, she was the first one off the stage.

He and Leah tried to draw her out on the way home, but she stared silently out the window.

"Do you want to take Bear for a walk when we get home?"

"I guess so."

His question hadn't inspired the enthusiasm he'd hoped it would. He drew in a breath, ready to give Olivia a short lecture on pet ownership and responsibility but suddenly he felt Leah's hand cover his. His brain barely had time to register the warmth and softness of her slim fingers before she pulled her hand away. It was almost as if she'd been able to read his mind.

The second the vehicle stopped in the driveway, Olivia was out the door and sprinting toward the house.

"Sometimes girls can turn on each other," Leah said. "Maybe she and her friends got into a squabble."

"*That* definitely isn't my area of expertise," Ben admitted. "In fact, I was about to give her a lecture in the car to help her snap out of it."

"I know."

He heard a smile in Leah's voice, not irritation. And he remembered the touch of her hand. "So, you've got another plan in mind?"

"Not at all." Leah shook her head firmly. "Olivia isn't the kind of person who lets things freeze up inside of her. She'll tell us when she's ready."

Two things struck Ben at that moment. He recognized that *he* was the kind of person who kept things frozen up inside of him and knew he didn't want that for his daughter. The other thing was Leah's casual use of the word *us*. That simple word linked them together in a way that made him wonder about the wisdom of letting Leah continue as Olivia's nanny.

He didn't want Olivia to get hurt when Leah got restless and decided to take another position—or when she realized that she wanted her own family to care for instead of someone else's.

Or maybe you're worried that Olivia won't be the only one who gets hurt if Leah leaves.

Ben shut that thought down as quickly as it had entered his mind. Leah Paxson was a loose cannon in his home. She changed his schedule without a second thought. She was partially responsible for the miniature grizzly living in his house and she'd unpacked her faith so that signs of it were everywhere, in spite of his hints that she keep it to herself.

But in a short time, she knew as much about his daughter as he did…if not a tiny bit more. And he had the uncomfortable feeling that she knew him, too.

"I'm ready to take Bear for a walk now."

Leah carefully wiped her hands on a dish towel and turned around. They'd been home for almost an hour and finally Olivia had sought her out.

"Would you like me to come with you?"

Olivia nodded.

Leah slipped her coat on and helped Olivia clip Bear's leash to his collar. It was obvious from the way he strained against it that he wasn't used to one.

"He'll have this figured out in no time," Leah said as they stepped outside. Bear began turning in circles to bite at the leash. "He's a smart dog."

"Do you really think so?"

"Here, we'll both hold on to him," Leah said, wondering at the mixture of hope and doubt she heard in Olivia's voice. "Of course he's smart."

"But he's a…mutt."

"A mutt?" Leah frowned slightly at Olivia's choice of words.

"That's what one of the boys at church said today. I

was telling my friends about Bear and he said that it was stupid to adopt a mutt."

Was that what had upset Olivia so much earlier in the afternoon? The quiet sniffle that followed Olivia's admission told her it was, but Leah sensed there was more to it than a boy insulting Olivia's new pet.

"Was that all he said?"

Olivia shook her head and Leah waited.

"He said that mutts are bad because you don't know what their moms and dads were like. He said that Bear would probably get mean and bite me."

Leah stopped on the sidewalk and knelt down beside Olivia, while keeping a firm hold on Bear's leash. "That isn't true, Livy. Just because a dog is a mixed breed doesn't mean that he's bad. In fact, one of the kids that I used to take care of had a book about dogs who were heroes and most of those dogs were like Bear."

Olivia looked up at her. "He said I'm a mutt, too, because I'm adopted and I don't know who my real parents are."

Now the tears spilled over and she burrowed against Leah's chest. Leah wrapped her arms around her, leash and all. Drawing a ragged breath, she prayed that she would find the right words to comfort Olivia. Children could be unbelievably thoughtless—she'd learned that as a child, too—but to have someone so cruelly comment on the fact that Olivia was adopted...

"Livy, look at me."

Olivia reluctantly lifted her head and used the sleeve of her jacket to mop at her face. She looked so forlorn that Leah's heart broke all over again.

"Do you remember what I told you when we prayed together the other night? That when Jesus is in your heart, He starts making you like Him? Now I want you to answer a question for me. What color are your eyes?"

"Brown."

"That's right. You got those beautiful brown eyes from someone." The memory of her mother's face rose in her mind. "But who put that little sparkle in them?"

Olivia thought for a moment. "Jesus."

Leah nodded. "And what color is your hair?"

"Plain old brown."

Olivia sounded a little disgruntled and Leah noticed her tears had dried up. "You inherited your *pretty* brown hair from someone, but who has every one of those hairs counted?"

"Jesus." A smile was beginning to touch the corners of Olivia's mouth.

"Exactly. That little boy who said those things wanted to make you feel bad, but you don't have to, Livy. The things on the *outside* of you, like the color of your eyes and how tall you'll be someday, are from your birth parents, but the things *inside* of you—in your heart—belong to God and He promises He'll keep working on them, just like your dad works on his special wood projects. You know that people recognize your dad's work even though he doesn't have his name spray-painted all over it. People are going to look at Olivia Cavanaugh and they're going to know who she belongs to because of who she is on the inside. And who she is is one of God's precious children."

Olivia was only seven but she was bright and Leah

knew that her heart was already tender toward the Lord. Hopefully she would understand.

"I love you, Leah," Olivia whispered.

"I love you right back, sweetheart."

Chapter Nine

Ben breathed a sigh of relief when he saw Bear charging up the driveway with Leah and Olivia close behind. They'd been gone almost an hour and he'd decided that if they weren't back within the next few minutes, he was going to go out and look for them.

Olivia was pink-cheeked and laughing as she tried to rein Bear in by his tangled leash. Apparently whatever had been bothering her had passed over like a summer storm. Another sigh of relief rushed through him. Just as Leah had suspected, Olivia had simply needed some time and space.

Leah. Her attention was focused on Olivia, so she didn't realize he was watching them. Even in the dusky evening shadows, her presence seemed to light up the front yard. She was wearing faded blue jeans and an old tweed coat that skimmed her knees, but still she somehow managed to look fresh and trendy. He could even hear her laughter as they watched Bear's antics.

The timer on the stove suddenly went off and he rapped on the window. He'd fixed two homemade pizza crusts with the dough that Leah had had rising on the counter, and the smell of the warm, yeasty bread had begun to permeate the house.

Leah looked toward the window and gave him a little wave, then said something to Olivia. Ben gave a low laugh as they sprinted toward the front door. He'd never seen Nanny Baker take part in a footrace against his daughter!

"Pizza!" Olivia shouted the word seconds later, jumping up and down when they came inside. Leah smiled at Ben over her head.

"Thank you," she said simply.

"Daddy says a guy should know his way around the kitchen," Olivia said, mimicking Ben's deep voice as she popped a piece of pepperoni into her mouth.

"How about you and I cut up the ingredients?" Leah suggested to Ben. "You take the pepperoni and I'll do the mushrooms."

"When are we going to get our tree, Daddy?" Olivia asked.

That's right. A Christmas tree. The beginning of the Christmas season. How could he have forgotten? "How about tomorrow morning?"

"It's Sunday." Olivia shook her head. "Leah and I have to go to church, don't we, Leah?"

Ben felt a stirring of resentment. Because he worked most Saturday mornings, Sundays were the only day he could truly call his own. He was able to sleep a little longer, make a big breakfast for Olivia and in the afternoon, play a knock-down-drag-out game of football with his brother and their friends. Except that lately the football tradition had come to a grinding halt, too, when Eli had started attending church again.

Leah hadn't responded to Olivia's plea and he flicked a glance at her, expecting to see a judgmental look on her face. Instead, he saw a look of complete understanding and it landed like a kick to his solar plexus. He didn't need her understanding.

"If you want a tree, we need to leave in the morning. That means no church."

He knew he was being unreasonable and the crushed expression on Olivia's face almost made him change his mind. Almost. "It's a long drive to the tree farm and you have school on Monday, so you can't do both."

"I guess we'll get a tree." Olivia glanced at Leah. "Are you going to come with us, Leah, or are you going to go to church?"

"Of course I'm coming with you," Leah said, sliding her arm around Olivia's slim shoulders.

"But you said they're going to start singing Christmas carols tomorrow and that's your favorite thing."

A smile tilted the corners of Leah's lips. "That is my favorite thing, but don't worry…I have an idea."

An idea. Suddenly Ben found himself wishing that he'd just let them go to church.

Later that evening, as he passed Olivia's room, he heard her talking. He assumed she was talking to Leah but when he peeked in, he realized she was alone. An odd assortment of things were scattered on her bedspread and he realized she was playing with the pieces of a nativity set.

She had an angel in her hand and lifted it high in the air. "'Do not be afraid. I bring you good news of great joy that will be for all people....'"

Ben realized she was practicing her lines for the Christmas program at church. She was the "head angel" who told the shepherds about the birth of Jesus and he remembered that it was right after she said her lines that she was supposed to sing a solo.

"'Today in the town of David a Savior has been born to you—He is Christ, the Lord...'"

Her voice faded away and he could see the frown of concentration on her face. Leah had told him that she'd memorized all her lines, but when he'd seen her earlier, she'd acted like she'd never practiced them before. And now, it appeared she was still having difficulty.

"'This will be a sign to you: You will find a baby wrapped in cloths and lying in a manger.'" Ben finished the verse quietly and Olivia twisted around to face him, her eyes wide.

"Do you know this story, Daddy?"

The surprised look on Olivia's face and the wonder in her voice filleted him open, right to the heart. For a second, he couldn't answer. When he did manage to summon some words, they didn't answer Olivia's question. "Where did you get all this?"

"Leah. She brought them from her apartment because these are her most special things, but when I told her we didn't have one, she said we could share hers this year."

Ben sat on the edge of the bed and picked up a shepherd. The piece was handmade ceramic and whoever had painted in the details hadn't been concerned with color or accuracy. The shepherd's hair blended into his robe and his feet were green. It almost looked as if a child had done it.

"You be him."

"What?" Ben blinked and Olivia lifted her angel toward the ceiling once again.

"You say his lines after I say mine," Olivia said patiently. She started again with "do not be afraid" and this time swept through her lines perfectly.

Then she looked at him. Closing his eyes, he let his memory take control. He'd heard this story all his life. It was only the past seven years that he had closed his mind—and his heart—to it. "Let's go to Bethlehem and see this thing…ah, that has happened, which the Lord has told us about."

Olivia grinned at him and clapped her hands. "Very good!"

Ben coughed. "Where is Leah, by the way?"

"She had to go to her apartment to get something," Olivia said. "She'll be home in time to tuck me in."

Ben wondered what had been so important to Leah that she couldn't wait until morning to retrieve it. He picked up a camel with blue hooves and Olivia giggled.

"He's weird, isn't he? But I didn't tell Leah that because I didn't want to hurt her feelings."

"You should get ready for bed. We've got a big day tomorrow if we're going to get our tree and you need your sleep." Ben dropped a kiss on the top of Olivia's shiny hair.

"I have to put these away first." Olivia started collecting sheets of tissue paper and used them to carefully wrap each piece of the nativity set. "Leah said she's had them for five years and she's moved ten times and never broken any of them."

Ten times? Ben couldn't imagine living such a vagabond existence. Except for the three years he and Julia were married, he'd lived in the same house all his life. What he didn't know was whether it was by choice that Leah had moved so frequently.

"How would you like to move that much?" Ben teased her in an attempt to shake away the uneasy feeling he had. If Leah was the kind of person who got bored easily and suddenly decided to leave, Olivia would be devastated. "I don't think there's a moving truck big enough to put all your things in."

"Leah says that she always asks God to give her to the kids who need her the most," Olivia said, her eyes serious. "And there's been a lot of kids who've needed her. But she'll stay here now."

"She will?"

Olivia nodded. "'Cause God knows *I* need her the most."

When Leah got back to the Cavanaughs', she saw Ben's silhouette in the yard and a massive shadow rolling at his feet. Bear.

Olivia's bedroom light was out and she glanced at her watch. She'd promised Olivia that she'd be back in time to tuck her in, but Ben must have put her to bed a little earlier. She'd needed to get some things from her apartment and then she'd called Anne Smith, who was scheduled to work with her in the church nursery the next morning, to tell her that she wouldn't be there. As the nursery coordinator, it was Leah's responsibility to make sure the nursery was fully staffed on Sundays mornings. There was a list of subs available for emergencies and she'd given Anne a few names of people to call if she felt she needed more help.

The two of them had ended up chatting longer than Leah had expected, but Anne, who worked at Tiny Blessings and was ordinarily quite shy, had shared some of the details of her upcoming wedding to Caleb Williams. Leah thought that the couple were an excellent match—Caleb's dark good looks and fun-loving personality was a perfect foil for Anne's golden beauty and gentle temperament.

On the drive back, with the passenger seat beside her loaded with an assortment of items from her apartment, Leah had felt a rush of loneliness.

Lord, this is getting difficult. I have feelings for Ben that I can't understand. Every time I'm with him lately I've been playing the same game Olivia does. It's so easy to pretend that we're a family. And Ben...he might think he's walked away from You, but I can tell he's hurting because of his decision. Find a way to reach him, Lord.

She parked her car in the driveway and immediately Bear loped over to investigate. The second she opened the door, he tried to climb into her lap.

"Down, Bear!" At the sound of her familiar voice, he whined in excitement.

"Don't even try." Ben's voice floated toward her through the darkness. "It's like pushing a ton of concrete." He came to her rescue and pulled Bear down.

"Time for bed, you big oaf."

"I noticed Olivia's light is off."

Was it her imagination or did a flash of guilt cross Ben's face? "We've got a long day tomorrow." He hesitated. "You don't have to miss church tomorrow, you know."

Leah's mouth dried up. "I don't mind."

"It's just that Olivia and I make a tradition out of cutting our tree down. It's something that my parents did when Eli and I were younger and they ruthlessly encouraged the next generation to continue it."

"Of course." Why had she assumed that she'd be welcome on a *family* outing? She thought of how disappointed Olivia would be when she found out that she wouldn't be going with them in the morning. Maybe as disappointed as she was, but there was a thread of something else in Ben's voice that had been impossible to miss. He was sending her a message. A reminder that she was the nanny. Hired help. Family traditions didn't include her.

She bent down to stroke Bear's soft ears so Ben wouldn't see the tears pooling in her eyes. "I remembered that I have nursery duty in the morning anyway. They're always shorthanded."

"I'm sure it will be nice to have a whole day to yourself tomorrow," Ben said. "You've been spending a lot of time with Olivia."

There it was again, that thread of warning. Maybe Ben had resented the thought that Olivia had sought her out and told her what had upset her that afternoon. She'd wanted to discuss it with Ben but now wasn't the time to bring it up.

"I never mind spending time with Olivia," Leah said. She reached into the car and pulled the duffel bag out. She wouldn't get to see Olivia's face when she opened the contents, but in her imagination she could see the little girl's mischievous smile. It was going to have to be enough.

God, is this how it's always going to be? Within a hug's reach of my daughter, but Ben tossing up walls that constantly remind me that I'm dispensable?

The words poured silently out of her heart but she made sure that Ben couldn't see the result of his polite dismissal. "Good night."

He was silent for a moment. "Good night, Leah."

The next morning, Olivia bounded into her room and landed in the center of the bed. She was dressed in denim overalls with a bright pink patch on the front pocket and a fleece cardigan. When she saw Leah slip her feet into a pair of high heels, confusion clouded her eyes.

"We're going to be walking in the woods, Leah! You can't wear those."

So much for her hope that Ben had been the one to explain that she wasn't going with them. "I'm going to church this morning, sweetie."

"But you said you were going with us!"

"I have to help take care of the toddlers in the nursery at church this morning."

"Then I'll help, too."

Ben, where are you? Leah silently wondered. "Your dad is looking forward to picking out a tree with you today. He'd be really disappointed if you changed your mind now."

"But you said you'd go with us."

She couldn't tell Olivia that she wasn't going because Ben didn't want her to. That would only cause a rift between the two of them, but her silence would tell Olivia that she didn't keep her promises. "Someone needs to take care of Bear today, too. We didn't think about him when we talked about leaving for the day. Puppies have to go outside a lot."

Olivia's lower lip trembled. "I guess so."

"Look, I have something for you." Leah retrieved the duffel bag by the dresser and sat down beside Olivia.

"What is it?"

"Church." Leah said the word cheerfully.

"Church?" Olivia peeked doubtfully into the bag.

"God wants us to worship with other people who believe, but church isn't a building. It's people. So you can take church with you." Leah pulled out a CD of popular Christmas carols. "You can sing along with these. And here's a Bible, only it's pictures instead of words."

"Wow." Olivia began to thumb through the book and Leah smiled.

"Like it?"

"I'd rather have you."

"This is a special day for you and your daddy," Leah said, pulling her into her arms and tickling her lightly. "You have fun and find the best tree."

"You'll help us decorate it, right? We always do that the night we get it."

She was afraid to promise even that now. "We'll see."

When Ben's truck pulled out of the driveway an hour

later, Bear gave a huge sigh and flopped down on the rug in the front hall.

"I know just how you feel," Leah told him.

She finished getting ready for church and gated Bear into the laundry room. She could feel tears simmering just below the surface and hoped that no one at Chestnut Grove Community Church noticed. Naomi Fraser seemed to have an internal radar for the hurting soul, so Leah decided the best thing would be to avoid her if possible.

"Hi, Leah."

"Good morning, Leah!"

She waved and smiled to the people who greeted her in the foyer and maneuvered through the crowded hallway as she headed for the wing where the nursery was located.

"Leah! I was hoping I'd see you this morning."

Naomi. Leah forced a smile. "Hi, Naomi."

"Is Olivia with you this morning?"

"No." Leah shook her head. "She and Ben went to cut their Christmas tree today."

"She seemed upset yesterday during practice and I was concerned. That little girl usually knows her lines by heart!"

"We talked about what was bothering her and I think she's fine now."

"You're a real blessing to the Cavanaughs," Naomi said, lightly squeezing Leah's arm.

A blessing? Not to Ben, that was for sure. As far as he was concerned, she was still there on a trial basis and that deadline was approaching fast. His comment the night before that she spent so much time with Olivia still weighed on her mind. It was obvious he was worried that Olivia was going to get too attached to her. But why hadn't he worried about that happening with Mrs. Baker? She'd been a part of their household from the time Olivia was an infant and Olivia still talked about her. She'd even written her a letter and told her that she missed her. How could he expect that Olivia wouldn't form a strong attachment to the woman who made her home with them?

"It's good to see Ben here lately, too," Naomi continued. "I've noticed he's been helping with the sets for the Christmas play."

"He wants to make sure everything is *perfect*." The words were out before Leah could stop them and Naomi looked surprised, then she smiled.

"I know from past experience when he's volunteered his time here that he's a bit of a perfectionist."

"That's the understatement of the year," Leah muttered.

"I'm sure you've been good for him in that respect."

Leah blinked. "Me?"

Naomi actually winked. "Yes, *you*. Now, time for me to lead the singing for the Sunday school classes."

Leah slipped on the white pinafore apron that all the nursery workers wore and ducked in the nursery, where Anne Smith was sitting in a rocking chair, toddlers spilling out of her lap as she tried to turn the pages of a storybook.

"You're here!" Anne's relief was evident and Leah laughed. "I called every sub on the list last night and no one could come in this morning. You are an answer to prayer, Leah Paxson."

Two children immediately attached themselves like barnacles to Leah's legs and she stepped between two little boys who looked like they were ready to go to battle over a wooden truck. She guided one of them toward the plastic workbench in the corner.

"You're really good at this," Anne said, shaking her head in awe.

"Practice, practice, practice." Leah sat down in the other rocking chair and was immediately covered in children.

"I'm glad you're here…but why *are* you here, by the way?"

"The Christmas tree outing is a family tradition." Leah tried to keep her tone casual but Anne gave her a sharp look.

"I thought they'd invited you."

"Olivia did, but Ben gave me the day off."

Anne's compassionate blue eyes studied her. "You really wanted to go, didn't you?"

Leah's throat closed. "I'd spend a whole day picking up LEGO blocks if I was with Olivia." And Ben. The truth of that thought seared her like the summer sun.

"It must be hard to love the children you take care of and then eventually have to give them up."

Not as hard as it had been to give up her daughter right after she was born. Leah figured that if she had the strength to do that, she could do anything. But now, at the thought of giving up Olivia all over again, she wasn't so sure anymore.

Chapter Ten

Something had been missing from the day. Or rather *someone.*

Even though Leah wasn't with them physically, she'd definitely made her presence known. Olivia talked about her constantly while they trudged around, looking for the perfect tree. Every time Olivia said her name, Ben felt a stab of an unwelcome emotion—guilt. He knew he had hurt Leah when he'd told her that finding the Christmas tree was a family tradition and had given her the day off. If she wasn't going to put up any boundaries with the amount of time and attention she gave to Olivia, he knew that he had to. It was in Olivia's best interests.

And yours? A voice inside mocked him.

Shaking the thought away, Ben glanced at Olivia, who had drifted off to sleep on the drive home as Leah's Christmas music played through for the fourth time. "Silent Night." "Angels We Have Heard on High." "O Holy Night."

He hadn't been prepared for the rush of memories that each one of those songs brought back. His mother had loved Christmas and managed to stretch the celebration of Christ's birth from one day to an entire month. A month filled with baking, decorating, visiting friends and family, Christmas carols. On Christmas Eve they would gather around the Christmas tree and his father would read the Christmas story from the gospel of Luke. That's why he knew it by heart. His parents had begun to plant the seeds of faith in his life from the moment the nurse had placed him in their arms.

But he hadn't done that with his own daughter. He hadn't been blind to the subtle ways his parents had communicated their faith to Olivia over the past seven years, but because they lived in Florida, their influence wasn't as great as his.

Now there was Leah.

The picture Bible that she'd given Olivia to page through was still in her lap.

You know this story, Daddy?

Her innocent question raked against his conscience again. Maybe it wasn't such a bad idea for Olivia to attend church and make her own decision about God.

Kids won't follow where a parent won't lead.

Great. One of his dad's famous euphemisms had come back to taunt him. Just what he needed! The truth was, he didn't know how to lead Olivia because he'd stepped off the path of faith, trying to make his own way.

His thoughts returned to Leah. What had she done during the day? Since she'd moved in with them, she hadn't received any personal phone calls in the evenings or on the weekends that he was aware of, and he wondered if she had any close friends. Even Nanny Baker had had a small group of women she'd gone to the Starlight Diner with once a week for coffee.

"Daddy? Are we almost home?" Olivia's eyes opened and she sat up sleepily.

"Just about."

Olivia yawned. "I want Leah to see our tree."

Ben glanced at his watch. It was almost time for supper. "Do you want to stop somewhere for a burger?"

"Nope. I just want to go home."

To Leah. The unspoken words were as clear as if she'd said them out loud. Frustration and amusement struggled for dominance inside Ben. Olivia was single-minded in her devotion to her new nanny—and Ben sensed that Leah's bond with his daughter was no less deep. That's what worried him.

Time to put up another boundary. "Well, I'm starving. Do you mind if we stop so I can get a burger and you can watch me eat it?"

Olivia was quiet for a minute. "No, that's okay, Daddy. We can stop."

The restaurant they chose was packed with people who must have had the same plan that they did. It took more than half an hour to get their food and Ben found himself missing the Starlight Diner's pleasant waitstaff, especially when Olivia accidentally spilled her glass of milk. Their waitress huffed and puffed and produced a stack of napkins as milk ran off the side of the table and pooled onto the floor at their feet. When Ben suggested a mop, she'd glared at him and informed him that she was too busy to get one.

When they got home and walked in the front door, Ben regretted their burger detour even more. He could smell baked chicken mingling with the aroma of something sweet.

Leah had made dinner for them.

"We already ate," he heard Olivia saying as he walked into the kitchen.

Strike two. Ben saw the dining room table set for three and the signs of a dinner that had been keeping warm for probably an hour or more. Leah tried to mask her disappointment but it was there in her eyes. He felt like a first-class jerk.

"I should have realized you'd stop somewhere," she said, her gaze seeking his and then moving swiftly moving back to Olivia. "I'll just put this in the fridge for tomorrow."

"You made Christmas cookies!" Olivia danced over to the counter and picked up a sugar cookie in the shape of a star, frosted yellow and decorated with colorful sprinkles.

Now Ben knew how she'd spent her afternoon. Preparing something special for their return. He groaned silently.

"I thought that you should have a treat while you decorated the tree this evening," Leah said.

"Can I have one now *and* later?" Olivia begged.

Ben nodded and Bear skidded across the kitchen floor as he came around the corner, wakened by the sound of Olivia's voice.

"I'm going to take Bear outside," Olivia announced around a mouthful of cookie.

"Don't feed him people food!" Ben said as Olivia broke off a piece of the star. She grinned and popped it into her mouth instead as they scrambled out the door.

Leah turned away and opened the oven door. "You can take a few pieces of chicken with you to work tomorrow. And some of the potatoes, too."

"I'm sorry, Leah. I didn't know you were planning to make dinner tonight."

Her back was toward him but he saw her shoulders stiffen. "I shouldn't have assumed."

So formal. The boundaries he'd tried to put into place had suddenly turned into a chasm between them that left him feeling unsettled. Unsettled but still reluctant to bridge.

"I better bring the tree in. Hopefully the ornaments will survive Bear's first Christmas." Ben waited a heartbeat but Leah didn't turn around.

When Ben left, Leah was able to breathe again. She leaned against the sink for support. She didn't know how much longer she could keep her feelings in check. She'd kept herself busy all afternoon, first by baking cookies to surprise Olivia and then by planning a nice dinner. It was her own fault that the chicken had baked right to the bottom of the roasting pan and the potatoes had turned out mushy.

While the cookies were in the oven, she'd curled up in a chair in the living room and read her Bible, but the peace she sought was elusive. Finally, she'd tried to empty her feelings on paper by writing in her prayer journal but had ended up doodling instead.

"Leah?" Ben's voice was muffled as he called her name.

There was a sudden loud *thump* and Leah hurried in the direction of the sound. Bear, the Christmas tree and Ben were all wedged together in the doorway. Bear whined pitifully.

"Don't ask," Ben growled as he peered at Leah through the branches.

Leah pressed her lips together to keep from smiling. She could hear Olivia giggling somewhere behind Ben. "Did you need something?"

"I'll tell you what I *don't* need," Ben said. "A sassy nanny."

"Sorry, that's the only kind we have available." Leah shrugged her shoulders.

Bear moved, the tree twisted and Ben gasped.

"Fine. I'll take her."

For a man as serious as Ben was, he was incredibly easy to laugh with, Leah realized in amazement. The tension she'd been feeling melted away and she knelt down beside Bear, who was cracking branches with every movement. She untangled his collar and freed him, then went to work on Ben's shoelace, which was wrapped three times around another one of the branches.

"Are you laughing at me?"

Leah looked up, only to see him scowling down at her. "Yes."

"I thought so," Ben muttered.

"Here you go." Leah unwound his shoelace and then retied it, the way she would have for one of her charges.

Together, they wrestled the enormous tree into the living room. By the time it was in place, they were both covered in fragrant needles.

Ben bent down to tie his shoe and paused when he saw she'd done it for him. "Double bunny ears?"

Leah felt her face grow warm. "Habit."

Ben grinned.

It wasn't often that she witnessed the full force of the charm that was held captive by his serious persona, but when it was unleashed, it had the ability to turn her insides into mush. His eyes crinkled adorably at the corners and a shadow of a dimple creased the corner of his mouth. But it was what happened to his eyes that took her breath away. Without the shadows in them—the ones that hovered like a cool mist over freshly tilled ground—he looked young and carefree. A reflection, Leah guessed, of the man he had been when he was married to Julia. And when he'd loved God.

Leah swallowed hard, frozen to the spot. All she could do was stare into those incredible brown eyes while every rational thought fled, leaving a jumble of scattered emotions.

She had known she'd fall in love with Olivia on sight. She'd loved her from the time she'd felt that first little fluttery kick inside. She'd loved her the first—and only—time she'd held her in her arms as a baby. She'd loved the precious memories she'd stored in her heart of those brief nine months…and when she'd seen her again, the love that she'd nurtured all these years had burst into bloom.

But she hadn't planned on falling in love with Ben.

She didn't even know what love looked like. Had occasionally wondered how she'd recognize it. When she was sixteen, she'd been a lonely teenager without a father, taken in by the flattering words and attention of someone who'd used that loneliness to further his own selfish needs. She had tricked herself into believing it was love. That it was forever. But now, when she looked at Ben, she had the first glimpse of what it could be like to grow old with someone.

Someone like Ben. No, not someone *like* Ben. Ben himself.

"Earth to Leah." One of Ben's eyebrows rose quizzically and Leah took a step away from him, as if that one small step would bring her heart back into line again. Not a chance. "Are you going to help us decorate the tree?"

Just as she was about to politely decline and escape to her bedroom to process the reality of her growing feelings for Ben, Olivia sailed in and rose on her tiptoes to wrap her arms around Leah's waist.

"Yup." She answered the question for her. "She is."

"I guess that settles it." Ben reached out and tousled Olivia's hair and for the first time Leah noticed how strong his hands were, how perfect they were, even though she'd seen the calluses on his palms. She forced herself to look away before he noticed that she was staring.

She and Olivia were given the task of bringing the boxes of ornaments out of the closet under the stairs, while Ben secured the tree in the stand. Olivia put in the Christmas carol CD and Ben shot her a wry glance from across the room.

Contrary to their concerns, Bear didn't bother the tree at all. He settled next to the rocking chair a few yards away and kept a wary eye on it, as if he was wondering when it would attack again.

"Livy, bring the box that says 'gold ornaments' over. Those go on first," Ben instructed.

Leah thought he was kidding until she saw that each box was labeled according to the color of the ornaments inside. Wow. After a few minutes of watching Ben study the tree like he would sight a rifle, she realized that in Ben Cavanaugh's world, there was only one way to decorate a Christmas tree. His way.

She decided to test her theory.

"Where does this skating penguin go?"

He glanced at her. "In the middle of the tree toward the fireplace."

"Uh-huh." She hung it at the bottom. Toward the sofa.

Olivia giggled.

"And the silver bell with the little Christmas carolers inside?"

"On the top near the back."

Leah winked at Olivia. Top near the front.

"Can we put the tinsel on this year, Daddy?" Olivia pleaded.

"Too messy."

Tinsel? Too messy? That was tinsel's exact purpose in life. To be messy and to cling to your clothes when you walked by and to clog up the vacuum cleaner.

Oh, Lord, help me, she pleaded silently as she realized that she was even beginning to love this side of Ben.

"I thought we threw that stuff away." He looked at

the boxes of tinsel like he would a piece of gum stuck to the bottom of his shoe.

"Grammy bought us more."

Ben frowned and Leah could read his mind. He was going to lecture his mother about future tinsel-buying excursions.

"I don't mind the mess..." Leah began just as the phone rang.

Ben excused himself to answer it.

Olivia looked at her hopefully.

Leah glanced at the boxes of silver tinsel that were in the box marked "miscellaneous," along with an odd assortment of decorations that included a fuzzy elf whose green felt suit was beginning to pill and a pine-cone snowman with pipe-cleaner arms. Apparently these were things that even Ben's logical brain couldn't quite categorize.

By the time Ben returned, the tree seemed almost animated from the gentle wafting of tinsel on the branches. But he didn't seem to notice. In fact, he didn't seem to notice anything, Leah thought in alarm. Somehow, the phone call had changed him. The shadows were back in his eyes and there was a tightness in his jaw.

"What do you think, Daddy?"

"I think it's beautiful," Ben said without even glancing at the tree. "And I think it's time for you to get ready for bed, peanut. It's a school day tomorrow."

"He's right," Leah said, wondering at the abrupt change in Ben's mood. "It's past nine o'clock and you still haven't had your bath yet."

Olivia looked ready to protest but then she nodded,

skipped to her father's side and planted a noisy kiss on his cheek. Leah guessed that her sensitive soul had picked up on the fact that her dad wasn't quite himself at the moment. With one last, longing look at the Christmas tree, she tangled her fingers together with Leah's and they went upstairs.

After she'd tucked Olivia in bed, Leah stood in the hallway, undecided what to do next. Ben hadn't come up to say good-night and she didn't hear a sound downstairs. No television. Nothing.

If she meant something to him…if they meant something to each other…she would have been at his side in a heartbeat. She would wrap her arms around him and lay her cheek against his chest and ask him what was wrong. But she didn't have a place in his life. Didn't have the right to go to him and encourage him to share his burdens.

A strange sound broke the silence and Leah followed it downstairs. She discovered Ben sitting on the sofa with her saxophone in his hands. That's what the noise was, she realized. He'd tried to blow into it.

"It's harder than it looks."

Leah suppressed a smile. "Six years of band."

"That explains it." He held it out to her and, wordlessly, Leah sat down and settled the instrument comfortably in front of her.

Ben's eyes were closed and she started to play. "Amazing Grace." She waited for Ben to tell her to play something else, but he didn't. When she dared to look at him, she saw that his eyes were closed. The pinched look around his lips had subsided a little.

She let the music say the words that she couldn't. And she prayed that somehow Ben would be able to understand.

Chapter Eleven

Ben let the music wash over him and, amazingly enough, the knots that were tangled up inside him began to ease slightly. He wasn't surprised that Leah chose a hymn; he was beginning to realize that she was an extremely intuitive young woman. She operated on a completely different plane than he did. Not bad, just different.

"My mom called and gave me her blessing to find my birth mother if I want to." Ben felt better now that he'd said it out loud.

He wasn't a musician but even he caught the off note as Leah's fingers faltered on the keys. She stopped playing and looked at him, waiting. Why had he confided in her? He shifted uncomfortably and exhaled a ragged breath.

"My friend, Kelly Young, recently discovered that years ago, the first director—Barnaby Harcourt—falsified some of the adoption records at Tiny Blessings." All the anger and confusion Ben was feeling rose to the surface again. Ever since he'd found out, he'd tried to keep himself busy and not allow his thoughts to dwell on what that might mean for his life. Until his mother's unexpected phone call had brought everything back. "There were quite a few of them that were changed— hers, mine…there were duplicate records and Kelly isn't sure which ones are the real ones and which are fake. I'd been told that my birth mother had signed a paper stating that under no circumstances should I try to contact her…ever. Not even if there was a medical emergency."

His parents had always been honest with him about the fact that he was adopted, but it wasn't until he was a teenager and had started to ask questions that they'd reluctantly told him about the "no-contact" clause. They hadn't wanted him to be hurt by the fact that even in a potentially life-threatening situation, his birth mother didn't want to be notified.

Any desire to meet her had died when he'd found that out. Although his parents couldn't give him any specifics about her, like how old she was or her family circumstances, he'd decided that if she wanted to completely forget that he existed, that was fine with him. Peggy and Tyrone Cavanaugh were his parents and they lavished enough love on him for ten sets of parents.

But after Kelly had told him that the no-contact clause may have been manufactured by Barnaby Harcourt, he'd been uncertain. And he didn't like being uncertain. He'd confided in Peggy and Tyrone, but for once they hadn't given him their opinion and the last thing he wanted to do was hurt them by trying to find his birth mother.

He thought he'd successfully squashed the inkling he'd been feeling to look more closely into his past... until his mom had told him she'd been praying about the situation and felt she needed to tell him that he had her blessing to search for his birth mother.

"But what if the no-contact clause was in the authentic document, not the fake, and you find a woman who doesn't want to have anything to do with you?"

Leah's quiet words were like an explosion in the room. She'd cut right to the heart of his fear. Rejection. Again.

"When Olivia was born and you and Julia adopted her, did you think that her birth parents were *rejecting* her?" she asked carefully.

He hadn't said the word "rejection" out loud, had he? No, once again it seemed that Leah could hear his thoughts. "No. Just the opposite. I was told they were teenagers and I thought that the mom must have been...brave. And strong. She could have made another choice." He tried to picture his life without Olivia, and the image was so dark and cheerless that he felt a cold tremor glide through him. "I thought of it more like an...offering, I guess. That she was giving Olivia a chance to have something she couldn't provide."

"Then why wouldn't you feel the same about the woman who gave you that same chance?"

"It was the no-contact clause, not even for a medical emergency." Ben rose to his feet restlessly and prowled the length of the room. "Apparently, I was an embarrassment. To shut down any future contact with me, she must have had a life she needed to protect."

"Or maybe a life she was protecting you *from.*"

"What?" Ben raked his hands through his hair and stared at her.

"Some kids grow up in terrible situations. Alcoholism. Drug abuse. Physical abuse. Maybe she lived in that kind of situation and didn't want her child to know. Ever. Maybe she wanted to give her child a chance at the kind of life *she* didn't have."

He'd never considered that possibility. How was it that he'd never considered that possibility? He was surprised to see tears in Leah's eyes and she seemed unaware of the fact that they were tracking uneven paths down her cheeks.

"I could hire a private investigator." It was something he'd been thinking about more and more over the past few weeks.

She nodded.

"And even if a private investigator found her, she wouldn't have to know."

"But you would."

"I would." The idea began to take shape in his mind and it didn't seem so shaky anymore. He needed to know if his birth mother had really signed that no-contact clause, and if she had, why? And if she hadn't…

Ben figured he'd cross that proverbial bridge when he came to it.

"All this turmoil." He forced a smile. "At least I don't have to deal with this with Olivia for a long time."

"What do you mean?"

"It was Olivia's birth mother's choice to have a closed adoption. We didn't know anything about her or her circumstances, other than the fact that she was a teenager. In a way Julia and I were both relieved that Olivia's adoption was set up that way. I guess that protective instinct works two ways. I have no idea what kind of person Olivia's mother is—whether she was a nice girl who simply made an error in judgment or someone who was promiscuous and her lifestyle caught up with her. Julia and I decided that if Olivia wanted to find her birth parents, we'd discourage her until she was at least twenty-one. That way the decision will be based on maturity and not emotion." Ben pushed his hands into his pants pockets and stared at the tinsel-covered tree.

He thought about his thirty-fifth birthday coming up in a few months and wondered if all these years his birth mother had been waiting…hoping…that he would contact her.

And maybe Olivia's birth mother was waiting, too. He hadn't considered that before. Olivia was so completely *his* daughter that he didn't think about a faceless stranger out there somewhere who was thinking about her. Wondering if they'd ever meet face-to-face.

He turned around but the sofa was empty. At some point, Leah had slipped out of the room.

Leah couldn't risk Olivia waking up and hearing her, so she curled into a tight ball on her bed, her knuckles pressed against her lips as she tried to contain the sobs that rolled through her body and demanded release.

Even though Ben had called her strong and brave, all she could focus on was his assumption that she'd been promiscuous. And because he doubted the character of a teenage girl who'd gotten into trouble, she knew he was hoping that Olivia's curiosity about her roots wouldn't lead to a decision to find her someday.

This is your punishment, she told herself. *That you did meet your daughter and you can't be her mother. You'll always have to pay for the consequences of your sin....*

The weight of the secret she was keeping from Ben pressed down on her.

This isn't the blessing from God you thought it was, is it? And now you're falling in love with Ben, too, and if he finds out who you are, you're never going to have a chance to be with Olivia...or him.

Leah sat up and turned on the light next to the bed. The shadows skirted into the corners and she rested her chin on her knees, trying to steady her breathing.

Her gaze suddenly rested on the nativity set Olivia had carefully placed on her dresser. Each figurine was in its exact spot, except for the wandering donkey, who Olivia delighted in moving from place to place. At the moment it was tucked behind the manger, where the tiny figurine of the baby Jesus was sleeping.

The truth wasn't in her chaotic thoughts and jumbled feelings, but right in front of her. God had a plan. Not just for mankind, but for *her,* Leah Paxson. From the moment she'd accepted the gift of His son and allowed Him access to every barren corner of her heart, her life was woven into His magnificent design.

Leah smiled. It wasn't the first time God had used that simple, imperfect nativity set to speak to her.

The nativity had been a gift from the children of the first family that had hired her right after she'd started working at Tender Care. They were twin girls whose parents were on leave from the mission field, and they'd hired Leah for the summer while they traveled and raised support for their next trip overseas.

The nativity set had been given to the girls to keep them occupied over the summer months and Leah ended up supervising the painting of the tiny figurines. After a few days of listening to the girls, she borrowed their children's Bible so she could read it for herself. On a hot summer day, Leah read the Christmas story while those ten-year-old girls patiently answered her questions about Jesus. Later that evening, it had been their mother, Rebecca, who'd listened while Leah had poured out her heart. She'd told Rebecca she didn't deserve God's love because of what she'd done and Rebecca had told her about God's grace and forgiveness.

She'd also warned Leah that there would be times in her life that she might doubt God's love, but to always remember the proof. He'd sent His Son...a gift of love and redemption to the world.

Rebecca, her husband and the girls went overseas again, but before they'd left they'd given Leah the nativity set. Leah counted it as one of her most precious possessions, not only because she loved the girls who had made it for her, but because it was a symbol of the way her life had changed.

Her thoughts drifted back to Ben. Squeezing her eyes

shut, Leah prayed for strength. And wisdom. She'd moved into Ben's home because she'd been certain that God had brought her back into Olivia's life for a reason. It was clear that Olivia needed—and wanted—a mother. So Ben bought her a puppy. Leah had seen right through that sneaky but strategic move! His actions recently had shown her that he was trying to keep her in her rightful place, yet he'd shared something with her tonight that she instinctively knew he hadn't shared with anyone else.

He needs You, Lord.

There was a quiet echo inside of her that she was afraid to dwell on.

He needs you, too.

With Olivia back in school after the Thanksgiving holiday, the house was quiet the next day. Ben hadn't lingered over breakfast, for which Leah was thankful. He'd given her a long, speculative look and then murmured a polite good morning before scooping up a cinnamon roll and heading out the door. Leah hadn't realized she'd been holding her breath until it whooshed out of her the second the door closed behind him.

Leah was glad she had Bear, whose presence brought some sparkle into her day. Wherever she was he wanted to be, and she took him for a long walk before jumping into her car to run some errands.

The secondhand store was first on her list. She was a regular customer there because she'd discovered that it was a veritable treasure trove for the vintage clothing she loved.

"Hi, Leah!" Gayle Tollie, the shop's owner, came out of the back room just as Leah paused in front of a section of bridal gowns. "I haven't seen you in a while."

"I have a new family," Leah explained, then bit her lip as the words she'd just spoken turned on her. "The Cavanaughs. Ben and Olivia." Her words tripped over each other.

Gayle looked meaningfully at the dress Leah was studying. "Something you've been keeping a secret?"

It took Leah a second to realize what Gayle was getting at and when she did, she let go of the sleeve and felt the satiny fabric slip through her fingers. "No, I'm making a costume for Olivia for the Christmas program. An angel costume."

"I've got some premade costumes over there," Gayle said, pointing to another corner of the store. "You won't have to do any sewing."

"I don't mind sewing. This one has to be special."

"Well…" Gayle moved farther down the rack and pulled out a dress that must have been made for a miniature bride. "How about this one? With some work, it should make a pretty decent angel."

The dress was white satin, the sleeves and hem trimmed with frothy lengths of organza. There were tiny pearl buttons up the back but the neckline was simple and rounded. Just the thing, Leah thought, for an angel.

"So, what do you think?"

"I think it's perfect."

"Do you want to see something else that's perfect? Follow me." Gayle motioned toward the storage room in the back of the store. "I thought of you the minute this came in. In fact, I'm not even going to put it out on the floor, I'm going to take it to a friend of mine who's an antique dealer and see what she thinks."

Leah followed her into the back room and Gayle went straight toward a plastic garment bag hanging high on a hook. Carefully, she unzipped it, revealing inch by inch the most beautiful vintage bridal gown that Leah had ever seen. It was a pale toffee-colored satin, simple in design but exquisitely detailed with hand-embroidery and seed pearls.

"I can't believe what people drop off here." Before Leah could react, Gayle was holding the dress up to her. "Look at this, Leah, I think it would fit you like a glove! Do you want to try it on?"

Leah stepped quickly away and held the miniature bride dress against her, almost like a shield. "No!"

Gayle blinked. "What's wrong?"

"I just don't have time today…besides that, do you see a ring on this finger?" Leah forced a laugh and held up her left hand.

"You wouldn't be the first woman to put a dress like this in her hope chest." The elderly woman shrugged her shoulders.

A hope chest. A charming but old-fashioned tradition that Leah hadn't started and knew she never would. She'd put her hopes and dreams into a young man once before and been brokenhearted. It wasn't until she'd put her hope in God that her life had started to make sense.

My hope is in You now, Lord, and if there is a man in my future, I'll let You pick him out this time. Ben's face flashed in her mind and she quickly shook the image away.

The bells on the front door suddenly came to life and Gayle quickly hung the dress back up. "Excuse me, sweetie. Duty calls." She hurried out of the storage room to greet her new customers.

Leah cast one more longing glance at the dress and then concentrated on finding the rest of Olivia's costume. An hour slipped by before she knew it and finally she went to the counter to have Gayle ring up her treasures.

"I think this is going to be the best angel costume I've ever seen," Gayle said as she slid the dress carefully into a bag. "I'd love to see it when it's done."

"Then come to Community Church on Christmas Eve," Leah said cheerfully. "Olivia will model it for you."

"You've been trying to get me to church for two years," Gayle huffed, but still she looked pleased by the invitation.

"And I'll keep trying until you show up."

Gayle sighed dramatically. "I give up. I'll be there."

"Ben Cavanaugh!"

Ben heard his name shouted from across the street and he saw the proprietress of the secondhand store waving frantically to him.

He waved back, ready to get into his truck.

"Ben Cavanaugh, do you have a minute?"

People started glancing their way and Ben hastily crossed the street. What was her name? Gwen? Gladys? Gayle. That was it.

"I can't believe I saw you this morning," she chatted. "I have a favor I need to ask of you."

"Ah…sure."

She held the door to her store open wide and Ben could only assume she needed advice on a carpentry project.

Gayle bustled over to the counter and picked up a dress. "Could you please give this to Leah? Tell her it's an early Christmas gift from a friend."

Even swathed in plastic, he could see that it was a bridal gown. "This is for…Leah?"

"That's right. The more I thought about it after she left, the more I realized that it was meant for her."

"This is for Leah *Paxson?*"

Gayle nodded. "I know she's just a tiny little thing and it might be too long, but she can always have it altered. Hope chest or not, she can save it for the big day. A sweetheart like that, it shouldn't be too long, now, should it? The men in Chestnut Grove aren't blind."

"No," Ben agreed absently, wondering why she thought he should be able to follow this particular conversation!

"Be careful with it, dear. It's fragile." Gayle patted the dress in satisfaction. "I wish I could see her face when she sees it again. It was made for her."

Ben glanced down at the dress draped over his arm and even a right-brained male like himself could see that she was right. The unusual color of the satin would bring out the gold flecks in her eyes. It was just like she was. Unconventional. *Beautiful.*

No way are you going down that road!

"But Leah isn't getting married." He had to state the obvious. Just in case…

"Not anytime soon, but eventually she will, don't you think?"

Yes, he did think. And the thought of Leah eventually getting married created a vague feeling of restlessness.

And general feeling of crankiness, although he wasn't sure why.

He knew he had to make a decision about Leah. Soon. For Olivia's sake, he told himself.

Chapter Twelve

When Ben got home from work that evening, there was a barefoot angel flitting around the living room.

"Look what Leah made for me!" Olivia twirled up to him, a miniature cloud in filmy white, complete with a set of transparent wings.

He reached out and straightened her halo.

"What do you think, Daddy?" Olivia tilted her head and the halo listed to one side again.

"I'm beginning to wonder if there is anything Leah can't do," Ben said under this breath.

"There isn't." Olivia grinned. "She can even sew buttons on your shirts if they fall off."

"Is that right?" Ben saw the gleam in her velvet brown eyes and instantly became wary.

"She thinks you smell good, too."

"What?" Ben's voice was strangled.

"She does. I wanted to put some of your perfume on Bear and Leah said that it makes *you* smell good but Bear wouldn't like it."

"It's cologne. Men's cologne," Ben corrected her, trying to process the fact that Leah thought he smelled good.

"She wouldn't let me put her perfume on him, either, 'cause then Bear would smell like flowers and he's a boy dog and he'd be embarrassed."

"Vanilla."

"Vanilla?" Olivia's nose crinkled.

The walls began to close in as his daughter's innocent gaze fixed on him. "That's what Leah's perfume smells like."

"So you like the way she smells, too."

"I didn't say that—"

"You're cheeks are getting kind of pink, Daddy."

"Windburn." He decided the safest thing to do was escape. "I better change my clothes before dinner."

He closed the bedroom door behind him and leaned against it, torn between a desire to laugh and throw something against the wall. If he'd had any doubt who his daughter had in mind to be her new "mommy," this latest conversation completely blew it away.

Now the question was, what to do about it?

Knowing Leah always planned dinner so that he could shower first, he had a few minutes to get his bearings again. Just in case Olivia launched a second campaign.

He towel-dried his hair until it was barely damp and then automatically reached for his cologne. And felt his face heat up again.

This time he could blame it on the steam from the shower. When they sat down to eat, he reached for the bowl of mashed potatoes but Olivia's words made him pause.

"We didn't pray yet."

He figured that if he did pray, it would definitely be for patience. He looked down at his plate while Olivia squeezed her eyes shut and talked to God like He was sitting at the table with them. Olivia took prayer very seriously and turned what should have been a simple blessing for the food into a lengthy dialogue that included parts of her day and specific requests.

"And, God, help me forgive Austin. Amen."

His curiosity got the best of him. "Who is Austin?"

"He's the boy at church who called me a mutt. Please pass the potatoes, Leah."

"A mutt? Why would he call you a mutt?"

"Because I'm adopted."

She said the words so matter-of-factly that for a moment they didn't register. When they did, Ben could hardly contain the anger that ignited inside him.

"Let me get this straight. He called you a mutt because you're *adopted?*" And this happened at church!" He cast an accusing look at Leah.

"It's okay now, Daddy. I talked to Leah about it. We're supposed to pray for our enemies, you know, even if we feel like kicking them. Right, Leah?"

Leah's response was a strangled sound. "That's right, sweetheart."

He wanted to argue the point but his mom and dad had taught him the same thing. Well, the praying part, at least. Although there'd been times he'd wanted to pray *and* kick his enemies.

"Did anyone ever tease you 'cause you were adopted?"

Olivia's question yanked him back in time, when he and Eli were just a few years older than Olivia. Some of the boys on the other football team had noticed the Cavanaugh boys had the same last name printed on the backs of their jerseys but looked nothing alike. Someone must have told them that they were adopted but that didn't prevent one of the boys, the one with the loudest mouth, from scoffing that if he was their dad, he would have dumped them off on someone else, too. Before he'd even finished the sentence, he'd been facedown on the grass with Ben kneeling on his back. Eli had simply walked away.

After the coach had peeled Ben off the other kid, Ben's punishment was to sit on the bench for the rest of the game. On the way home, his dad had told him much the same thing that Leah had told Olivia. Holding on to anger would only hurt *him* in the long run, Tyrone had said. Pray for that kid, his dad had urged. He's the one who's really in trouble.

"Just once," Ben answered Olivia's question and remembered now that he *had* prayed. And surprisingly enough, he could still remember how good it had felt to turn his anger and bitterness over to the Lord. But that was a time in his life when he was sure that God answered prayer.

With a surge of frustration, Ben realized that lately he'd been remembering a lot of the things his parents had taught him about God. Things that he'd accepted and believed without question…until Julia died. And the fact that he was thinking about God again at all…well he put the blame squarely where it belonged—on the slim shoulders of the young woman sitting at his table!

He didn't want to revisit his past. "You didn't tell me what happened at school today."

Fortunately, Olivia accepted his simple response to her question and turned the dinner conversation to school and the upcoming Christmas play.

"Are you going to need help with the set again this week?" Ben asked Leah, when Olivia stopped talking long enough to eat a dinner roll.

Even with Olivia barely taking a breath between sentences, he noticed that Leah seemed rather quiet. He wondered if her mood was connected to the way she'd snuck out on him during their conversation the night before.

Now, she looked up at him and their eyes met across the table. "We've got practice two nights this week but Mrs. Fraser mentioned our practice on Saturday is going to be rescheduled because of the tree lighting ceremony at the mayor's mansion."

Ben nodded. The Christmas tree lighting ceremony at the mansion was a holiday tradition in Chestnut Grove. Ninety percent of the town showed up for the festivities, which included a tour of the mansion and hot chocolate and cookies afterward. He'd taken Olivia every year because it was something that Julia had enjoyed, but now he viewed it more as an opportunity to make business connections. It was the only way he could reconcile it with the emptiness he felt for all things Christmas-related.

"You're coming with us, right, Leah?" Olivia asked the question between bites of mashed potatoes.

"I'll have to check my calendar," Leah said, but her smile seemed forced. "I've got a lot of work to do on the sets before the dress rehearsal and I may have to take advantage of the peace and quiet to get some work done."

"You have to come!"

Ben knew what was behind Leah's reticence—he was. Apparently when he'd given her the day off so he and Olivia could continue the family tradition of cutting their Christmas tree, she probably assumed that any future outings excluded her, too.

"If Leah has plans, peanut, then you and I will just have to go. Like always."

He wasn't prepared for the sudden clatter of Olivia's fork against her plate. There was suddenly a strange child sitting at his table. A child whose chin jutted forward stubbornly and whose eyes flashed gold sparks at him.

"Daddy, you keep ruining it!" Her chair scraped against the floor as she rose to her feet.

He hadn't a clue what she was talking about. "Olivia, what are you talking about?"

A dramatic huff was the only response he got before his cheerful, ordinarily well-mannered child, stomped out of the room.

He turned to Leah. "Do you have any idea what it is that I keep ruining?"

Leah was afraid she did. Olivia wanted to pretend that Leah was her mother. She wanted the three of them to do the things that families did. Like attend the Christmas tree lighting ceremony. The irony of the situation wasn't lost on her. She really *was* Olivia's mother and Ben frequently reminded both of them that they weren't a family.

"I think that Olivia likes us to do things together." That seemed a safe enough reply.

"She's getting too attached to you."

Leah's heart rate kicked up a notch. "She was attached to Nanny Baker, wasn't she?"

"It's different with you." Ben stared at her intently.

"Olivia is getting older," Leah said, careful to keep her voice even, although panic was starting to claw at her insides. Was he going to fire her right there at the dinner table? "It wouldn't be unusual for her to bond with the woman who's taking care of her."

"Bond." Ben repeated the word. "I think you and I both know it's more than that."

Leah held her breath. So much for her hope that Ben wouldn't see through Olivia's matchmaking schemes. It was getting difficult for her, too, especially when she acknowledged her growing feelings for Ben. But to leave them…

"I've got to think about this some more," Ben said. "What do we have left on our trial period? Two weeks?"

"A little bit more." Two weeks, twelve hours and thirty-six minutes.

"All right. Before Christmas." Ben stood up and headed toward the door. "I've got some work to do but if Olivia needs any help with her homework, she can let me know."

Leah could read between the lines. *Me parent, you nanny.*

Lord, I'm not going to quit praying for Ben, she prayed silently. *But right now I really want to kick him.*

* * *

When she got back home after dropping Olivia off at school the next morning, she found a trunk sitting in the middle of the living room floor with a note taped to the top.

Forgot to give this to you yesterday. You can keep the trunk.
Ben

The trunk was similar to the one at the foot of her bed, only this one was smaller than a blanket chest. The top was curved and the hardware was a soft antique bronze.

She opened the trunk and the scent of cedar wafted out. Folded carefully inside was the wedding dress from the secondhand store.

Overwhelmed, Leah sat back on her heels. Gayle, sweet schemer that she was, must have given the dress to Ben to surprise her. She could only imagine what Ben must have thought! And why had he put it in a cedar chest instead of just tossing it over the back of the sofa?

A hope chest. Gayle's words came back to her and Leah exhaled to relieve the pressure building inside. The guilt over her past swept down like an avalanche, telling her that she didn't deserve to have hope.

She closed her eyes and prayed through it until the weight of the lie dissipated—replaced with truth. Rebecca had told her to fight those lies with Scripture, just like Jesus had done when the enemy taunted Him in the desert. Those words of wisdom had become as precious as gold over the years.

"Leah, when doubts come, deal with them quickly. Don't give them a chance to take root. Treat them like the weeds they are and yank them out or they'll start to take over," Rebecca had told her. "There is a verse in Philippians you should write on a card and memorize. It starts out by saying 'whatever is true.' Sometimes people skim right over that word and concentrate on the rest of the verse, but you can't. A lot of the things the enemy throws in your path to make you stumble are lies and the only way you can fight lies is with *truth*."

Clinging to the truth, Leah waited until the familiar feeling of peace washed everything else away. When she opened her eyes, her attention shifted from the dress to the trunk Ben had made. She ran her fingertips along the edges, in awe of the craftsmanship. He had a gift. There were only a few pieces of his handmade furniture in the house, leading her to the assumption that he didn't make time to do something that he enjoyed. He scheduled his days too tightly to leave room for a hobby, although Leah had no doubt he could make a living just selling the things he created out of wood.

She planned to give them back. Both of them. The trunk and the dress. But maybe…

Leah couldn't resist the urge to pull the dress out and look at it one last time. What would it hurt to just try it on? Just for fun? She went upstairs to her bedroom, slipped out of her blue jeans and sweatshirt and shimmied into the dress.

Gayle had been right. It fit her like a glove. The gown fell just past the tips of her tennis shoes and the color was perfect. She twirled around three times, enjoying the sweep of the fabric against her bare legs and then laughed at the silliness of it.

"Okay, Cinderella, the clock is about to strike twelve...."

The doorbell rang just as she reached around to unzip the dress and she grabbed a handful of satin, hiking the dress up to her ankles as she hurried downstairs to answer it.

A delivery truck was idling in the driveway and the driver was standing at the front door with a package for Ben.

Leah eased halfway out the door, hoping that the driver wouldn't notice what she was wearing. She signed for it and breathed a sigh of relief as he strode back down the sidewalk without a flicker of a change in his expression.

She didn't notice Bear until he butted the door open and bolted outside, eager to play.

"Bear! Get back here!" Leah hissed.

He ignored her and sniffed a crooked path through the grass.

"Bear, I mean it!"

His massive head lifted and he grinned at her, his tongue a bright pink ribbon unfurling from the side of his mouth.

Leah took a cautious step outside. Bear, ecstatic that he'd managed to lure her into a game, took several bouncy steps in the opposite direction.

"No treats for you today," Leah muttered.

She gave up and went after him. The chase was on.

Chapter Thirteen

Ben couldn't believe his eyes. Just as he turned the corner, half a block from home, he saw Bear streaking down the sidewalk. Just a few yards behind him, in hot pursuit, was Leah.

Wearing a wedding dress.

He pulled over to the side of the street and pushed open the passenger door. And whistled.

Bear veered off course and launched himself into the cab of the truck. Leah skidded to a stop several yards away and stared at him.

He'd wondered what she'd look like in that dress.

By the time he'd remembered that it was still in his truck, Leah had gone to bed for the night. He'd brought it into the house and figured that it needed to be preserved in something better than a thin plastic garment bag.

Then he'd remembered the trunk. It wasn't a practical size. It was too small for storing quilts and the curved top made it an impractical shape to slide under a bed or chest of drawers. He'd made it when Olivia had had the chicken pox and he'd taken a week off from work to help Mrs. Baker take care of her.

Making wood furniture was something he loved to do but after Julia died, he'd had the added responsibility of building up a name for himself in the carpentry business, so it was something that he'd put aside. Even though his mom still occasionally hinted that she'd love a new bookcase, he still couldn't bring himself to make the time.

The trunk, however, had been born out of worry. Olivia's mild case of chicken pox had turned into pneumonia and during the pockets of time during the day when she'd slept, he'd needed something to keep his mind and hands busy. Once she started getting better, the trunk had served its purpose. He'd pushed it into a corner of his room and figured someday he'd figure out what to do with it.

Why he'd thought of the trunk when he'd lugged the wedding gown into the house the night before, he didn't know, but the dress had fit inside like it had been made for it.

That was when his imagination had conjured up an image of Leah wearing it.

But his imagination hadn't done that image justice. There was no way it could have. Not when the reality was a breathless Leah standing on the sidewalk with wind-tossed hair and tennis shoes peeking out from beneath the hem of the gown. Even in the distance between them he could see the laughter in her eyes, the bloom of color in her cheeks.

If he'd have told anyone that Leah Paxson was dangerous, they would have told him he was crazy. She probably weighed a hundred pounds soaking wet and the top of her head barely grazed his shoulder. But dangerous she was, and the moment their eyes met across the sidewalk, he knew why. Up until now, he'd been able to deny the confusing mix of emotions he felt whenever she was in the vicinity. He'd been able to keep a tight rein on the fact that Leah was his daughter's *nanny.* An exasperating, saxophone-playing rule breaker who delighted in rearranging his schedule and who'd covered his Christmas tree with tinsel.

And even though she'd never quite looked like a nanny, now she looked like a…bride. Before he could shut them down, his traitorous thoughts transported her from the sidewalk to the stain-glassed sanctuary at Chestnut Grove Community Church.

Even though he volunteered to help with certain projects at the church, he tried to avoid it as much as possible. The good memories he'd once associated with it had been replaced years ago with one dark one—Julia's funeral. But now, instead of the memories of a crowd of people gathered around him to express their sorrow, the only thing he could see was Leah waiting at the altar for her bridegroom.

That's what made her dangerous.

Without a word, he nudged the accelerator with his foot and drove the short distance to the house. By the time he pulled into the driveway, Bear had successfully fogged up every window in the truck.

Leah was walking toward him at a much slower pace than the one he'd just witnessed.

He jumped out of the truck and waited for her to reach him. "Interesting choice of active wear," he said. "I'm not sure it'll catch on, though."

"No?" Leah pretended to consider the comment and smoothed the wrinkles out of the skirt.

"No." Ben tried not to notice the way the satin accentuated her gentle curves. The ones he'd never noticed before.

"I had to try it on just once, before I give it back to Gayle."

"She called it an early Christmas gift."

"She's sweet that way but one of the antique shops specializes in vintage clothing and I happen to know that she could get quite a bit for a dress like this in mint condition."

Bear let out a sharp bark to remind them that he'd been forgotten and Ben rolled his eyes. "Better grab on to something solid or he'll knock you over. Remind me again why we got this animal?"

"For Olivia."

"Right. Olivia." Ben opened the door of the truck and used it as a shield as Bear soared out of the cab. His moment of indecision, when he was trying to decide whether to take the sidewalk or the neighbor's hedge, cost him. Ben grabbed his collar, winced as a sharp pain radiated down his arm when Bear lunged, and towed him toward the house.

"It's a beautiful trunk," Leah said, following him inside. "Where do you want me to put it?"

"You can keep it."

Leah was silent for a moment. "Was it Julia's?"

He wondered why she'd asked. "No. It wasn't anyone's. But now it's yours."

It wouldn't have mattered if it had belonged to Julia, he realized. Julia would have liked Leah. Although he and Julia had been similar in temperament, Julia always seemed to seek out people who were spontaneous and made her laugh. She even had a name for them. *Joy seekers.*

"I love people who trust that God is working even when life doesn't make sense," she'd frequently told him. "I want to be like that."

And she had been, Ben realized. When she'd been diagnosed with ovarian cancer, her relationship with God had deepened at the same time that his had crumbled. What had made the difference? He wasn't sure he wanted to shine a light on his soul and find out.

"Ben? Why do you have a T-shirt wrapped around your arm?" Leah asked suddenly.

"Jonah decided to knock a wall down and I didn't get out of his way fast enough. That's why I came home. The woman whose library we're working on almost fainted when she saw me, so I thought I'd better come back here and take care of it."

"I'll be right back." Leah called Bear into the laundry room and then returned without him. "Let me have a look."

"It's just a scratch."

"Well, the scratch is soaking through that dirty T-shirt you're using as a tourniquet," Leah said. "Come into the kitchen."

Why did women make such a big deal out of things like this? Ben wondered. So a nail grazed his arm when he tried to catch the wall with the top of his head!

"At least let me get you a Band-Aid, tough guy."

"I probably will need a Band-Aid." That they could agree on. He wouldn't have done anything to it if Mrs. Wagner's face hadn't gone as white as the paint she'd picked out for the walls when she'd seen him. Burying a sigh, he followed Leah.

It was going to need stitches. Probably four.

Leah, having taken care of three boys between the ages of four and ten, was well-acquainted with stitches. Two foreheads, one knee, a chin and the bottom of a foot in less than twelve weeks. She'd watched the boys for an entire summer while their mother took a vacation by going back to work, and she'd gotten to know the emergency staff at the hospital so well they'd given her a box of chocolates and a first-aid kit when it was time for her to leave.

Her stomach rolled as she saw the gaping wound on Ben's arm and she quickly tossed the T-shirt in the sink.

"You need stitches."

"I don't need stitches." Ben gritted his teeth as her fingers gently prodded the gash in his skin.

"When was your last tetanus shot?"

"I don't need a tetanus shot!"

"Maybe you didn't before, but the minute you wrapped that dirt-encrusted shirt around it, you pretty much sealed the deal."

"Ow!"

"Hurts, doesn't it?"

"*A little.*"

"Men."

"What do you know about *men?*" Ben's breath hissed between his teeth when she took a wet cloth and pressed it against the cut.

"A lot," she retorted, watching as the white cloth immediately turned pink, then red. She couldn't believe he'd been calmly talking to her in the living room while he was bleeding to death. If she hadn't suddenly noticed the shirt wrapped around his arm, he probably would have just slumped at her feet!

"A lot?" he repeated softly.

"Okay, next to nothing." She had to admit it. "But I watch television."

"I'm not even going to go there," Ben said and winced again. "Television being such an accurate portrayal of real life. Just slap the Band-Aid on and let me get back to work."

"I'll drive you to the hospital."

"Leah, you just got blood on your sleeve." Ben pulled away from her.

Leah glanced down at her arm and saw a few drops of crimson on the fabric. "Here, hold this against the cut for a few minutes. I'm going to change quick and then I'll go to the hospital with you. You can even drive if that sits better with your macho carpenter image."

"I can't believe I hired you to be a good influence on my daughter," Ben breathed. "You're a five-foot-two tyrant."

Leah tilted her head and looked up. "Five-foot-three."

Her hand slid down the length of his muscular forearm and she gave his fingers a comforting squeeze, then immediately realized what she'd done the minute his expression changed.

She might not know a lot about men…okay, next to nothing—and what she did was negative so she tried not to let it unduly color her feelings about them in general—but she saw a look in Ben's eyes that she'd never seen before.

A flicker of admiration. A flicker of…*like*. In spite of his less than flattering description of her personality, there was a super-charged moment between them that weighted the air and kept their fingers touching for a millisecond.

Until Ben pulled away. The warmth in his eyes disappeared. "I pay you to take care of Olivia, not me."

By Wednesday, Leah was convinced she'd imagined the look in Ben's eyes. He'd barely spoken to her other than to tell her not to keep dinner waiting for him at night. His excuse was that he and Jonah had to finish the library so the Wagners could host their annual Christmas party and they'd gotten behind schedule because Mrs. Wagner had decided to have them replace the wobbly banister on the staircase, too.

He came home just in time to spend half an hour with Olivia before she went to bed and then he disappeared into his office. She wanted to ask him what he'd decided to do about his birth mother. Had he hired a private investigator? She wanted to know if his arm was healing. She'd been wrong about the stitches. He hadn't needed four, he'd needed six. The next day, an E.R. nurse had called to ask how he was doing and mentioned it. Leah hoped he'd gotten a tetanus shot, too.

She heard a tentative knock on the connecting door between her and Olivia's rooms and finished tying her shoes.

"Are we going now, Leah?" Olivia's gamine face peeked in, then she bounced into the room.

"In a few minutes." Leah had changed into her old paint-covered blue jeans and a black cable knit sweater that she'd had since high school, but she still needed to fix her hair.

Olivia went right over to the nativity set on the top of the dresser and began to play with the donkey. "Is Daddy going to help you tonight?"

That was another question she wanted to ask Ben but was afraid to. He wasn't the only one who was behind schedule. A bout of strep throat had recently swept through the youth group, causing a serious dent not only in Leah's faithful set crew but also in the kids who were helping Naomi with costumes. Leah had been going back and forth between painting, outfitting a small herd of sheep and sewing new sequins and trim on the three wise men's robes. She could really use his help but not once had he surprised her by showing up at the church to help.

"I don't think so." She pulled her hair back and wound it quickly into a messy bun at the nape of her neck.

"Is he working late again?"

Leah heard the thread of disappointment in Olivia's voice and it squeezed her heart. She knew she wasn't the only one who missed their dinners together every evening. Didn't Ben see that by distancing himself from her, he was hurting Olivia, too?

"I think so. Maybe some night we'll just have to bring dinner to him and Jonah. What do you think about that?"

"Tomorrow!"

Leah laughed. "We'll see. I don't think we'll surprise him this time, so I'll find out what night will work best."

She gave Olivia a one-armed hug as she reached for the tiny bottle of perfume on the top of her dresser.

"Can I have some?" Olivia offered her wrist and Leah sprayed a little one. "Daddy likes this kind."

"What?"

"He likes this kind. He told me you smell good. Like vanilla." She buried her face against Leah's sweater. "You do smell good. Like cookies."

"Thanks," Leah murmured, her breath hitching slightly. Had Ben really told his daughter that he liked the scent of her perfume? It was confusing, especially because Ben had been careful to avoid her since the day he'd witnessed her wearing a wedding gown and sprinting after Bear. She resolutely snuffed out the spark of hope that had flared in her with Olivia's innocent declaration.

Or had it been innocent?

She was getting to know her daughter very well and the mischievous smile dancing near the corner of her mouth was a dead giveaway. She was up to something.

They heard a door close downstairs. Olivia gave a delighted shriek and disappeared out the door. Leah doubted her feet even touched the stairs.

Glancing at her watch, Leah realized they were going to be late for practice if they didn't leave within the next few minutes. She found everyone in the living room moments later. Olivia was sitting contentedly in her father's lap while Bear sprawled at his feet, nibbling on his shoe laces.

"I'm ready, Leah," she announced, shifting her weight as she started to jump down.

Leah saw a flash of pain on Ben's face.

"Honey, be careful of your dad's stitches," she warned quickly.

"I'm sorry!" Olivia was immediately repentant and swung around carefully to plant a kiss on Ben's tanned jaw.

Ben's expression was almost comical as he stared at her and Leah's sense of humor teased its way to the surface. "He has six of them," she said in a stage whisper. "And they take a while to heal."

"You take good care of us." Olivia turned to her father. "Doesn't she, Daddy?"

Leah groaned silently. There was that smile again. She needed to have a long overdue talk with a certain little girl! She hustled Olivia into her jacket and out the door but it wasn't until later that she realized that Ben hadn't answered the question.

Chapter Fourteen

Ben's conscience played tug-of-war with him all evening. He picked up the novel he was reading and tried to lose himself in the espionage plot, but when he realized he'd just reached chapter five and couldn't remember anything that had happened in chapter four, he tossed it down impatiently.

Bear whined and he glanced up. The dog had ventured too close to the tree and static electricity had performed its duty—the tinsel had attached itself to his fur like a magnet.

"Come here." Ben couldn't help but smile. "That's why tinsel is a menace, boy. It never stays put."

Bear trotted over to him, trailing ribbons of silver like a Christmas parade float and stood patiently beside Ben's leg as he removed the offending decorations.

"Wow. This is a sight you don't see every day."

Ben scowled at his brother, who stood in the doorway grinning. "How did you get in?"

"The butler." Eli shrugged and wandered into the living room.

Ben felt Bear shudder in excitement so he kept a firm grip on his collar until Eli crouched down and met the dog's intelligent gaze, eye-to-eye.

"I heard you got a puppy," he said, scratching Bear's ear and earning his undying devotion. "Where is it?" He looked expectantly around the room.

"Funny." Ben rolled his eyes. "You're petting it, you idiot."

"This looks more like a government experiment gone awry...a tank covered in fake fur—"

"I get it." Ben lifted one hand to stop his brother's stand-up comedy routine. "Why are you here?"

Eli dropped into the leather recliner. "Do I need a reason?"

"Considering the fact I haven't seen you since Thanksgiving and now you show up on my doorstep...yes." Even as he spoke, he knew he couldn't put all the blame on Eli. Ever since Eli had found his footing with God again, Ben had felt a barrier between them—one he'd put into place.

"I'm a newlywed," Eli reminded him.

Ben flushed. "Right."

Eli's expression changed with the speed of a daily calendar. "Mom's worried about you."

He was afraid of that. He hadn't talked with her on the phone since she'd dropped the blessing bomb on his head. He had two phone numbers for private investigators written in his planner and hadn't called either one. He still wasn't quite sure what was stopping him.

"I'm fine. I just haven't decided yet."

"Whether to track down your birth mother?"

Ben saw the compassion in his brother's eyes and felt another fissure in the walls he'd put up. Walls that even his own family hadn't been able to breach. "It's stupid, isn't it? This need to know?"

"No."

Eli's simple response volleyed the conversation right back into Ben's court.

"Are Mom and Dad…" He struggled to find the right word.

"Hurt?" Eli shook his head. "When Mom prays about something and gets the go-ahead from God, she listens. Like she always says, faith first, feelings…"

"Follow." Ben finished the phrase. Another one of the things he'd been taught. One of the many lessons he'd forgotten that had been air-bubbling to the surface lately.

"You know it." Eli pulled a stray strand of tinsel from the bottom of Bear's paw. "That's quite a tree you've got there. Did you go to McAllister's Tree Farm?"

"Me and Olivia." Ben grasped at his brother's abrupt detour from the path their conversation had been going. He wasn't ready to deal with it at the moment.

"And Leah?"

"No." Ben still felt a stab of guilt over that afternoon. Leah's burned dinner. The Christmas cookies waiting for them. The hurt in her eyes that she couldn't quite conceal.

Eli flashed a speculative look at him. "Doesn't Olivia like her?"

"Just the opposite. I think she's trying to play matchmaker between the two of us," Ben said darkly.

Eli obviously didn't see the concern there because he started to laugh.

"She thinks she needs a mother," Ben added.

"She does."

Ben gaped at him.

"But maybe not as much as you need a wife."

The bittersweet memory of Julia's pretty face returned and Ben's throat closed. "I had one of those."

"And Julia wouldn't have wanted you to close yourself off from love," Eli said. "She told me before she died that she was afraid this would happen."

Ben felt the air slowly being squeezed out of his lungs. "What would happen?"

"You tried to hide it, but she could tell that your faith took a major hit when they found the cancer. She could see that you hid your pain inside your work and she was afraid that someday you'd just disappear inside of it."

"I've been there for Olivia."

"You're a great dad."

Ben had a feeling Eli wasn't finished. "But?"

"But I stood next to you when Olivia was a month old and you dedicated her to the Lord. You promised to do more than just love her, you promised to teach her to love the Lord. And I promised to help you."

"That was seven years ago." Ben heard the anger seep into his tone, but at the moment he couldn't control it. Inside, his emotions were shouldering against the wall he'd built and it was shuddering under the weight.

"I had my own issues with God that I needed to work through," Eli said. "Julia was a believer and so are you, and even though you've withheld your trust, God hasn't withheld His love. It's been there all along. Someday you and Julia will see each other again and you need to keep your promise to Olivia so that she can have the hope of heaven, too. It's the only thing that beats death—knowing that death isn't the end of life. We don't grieve like those who have no hope, remember?"

Eli's paraphrase of the verse that the minister had read during Julia's funeral seared his soul. He'd wanted to shout at the guy to shut up. How could he talk about hope when everything Ben had hoped for—a wife, a family, a comfortable life—was lying in fragments at his feet?

Eli rose from the chair and tossed a pillow at Ben. It hit him square in the chest and Ben thought for a moment that it was going to go right through the gaping hole his brother's words had just opened up. It bounced off instead and Bear landed on it with a delighted woof.

"Open your eyes, big brother. Quit focusing on what you think God's taken from you and see what He's given you instead. I think you'll be surprised."

"Are you talking about Leah?" Ben managed suspiciously.

"Actually I was talking about Olivia," Eli said, one eyebrow lifting. "But you said it, not me."

"Good night." Ben growled the words around the emotion still clogging his throat.

Now there was amusement mingled with the compassion in his brother's eyes. "I'm praying for you."

He'd heard the words many times over the past seven years and he'd successfully blocked them out as the overused, trite expressions of Christian love he thought they were. But suddenly, faced with the truth of that love reflected in his brother's eyes, gratefulness burst through him like a broken water main.

"Thanks," he whispered.

Eli clamped a hand on his shoulder. "What's a brother for?"

"Leah, you are a wonder."

Leah bloomed under Naomi's warm praise as the older woman inspected the costumes that Leah had finally finished the evening before. "I'm glad I could help."

"Help?" Naomi chuckled. "I think you've single-handedly saved the Christmas program this year. Who knew that a box of sheep costumes were going to be misplaced so they'd need to be *replaced?* Or that the director of the program was going to end up with strep throat? Well, of course God knew, that's why He gave me you."

"You look like you're feeling better." Leah had stopped by the Frasers to pick up the box of costumes three days ago and a feverish Naomi had answered the door at noon, still in her nightgown and slippers. It had been Leah who'd urged her to go the doctor and get a strep test.

"John threatened to put me under house arrest if I didn't stay in bed and do anything but read," Naomi said. "I told him I could sew costumes while I was horizontal but he wouldn't let me. That's why I ended up calling you."

Leah was glad she had and for the past few nights she'd been sewing miniature sheep costumes out of fake fleece, attaching felt ears to headbands and letting the hems down on the shepherd's robes because this year's crop of shepherds were taller than she was.

"I suppose I'll see you tonight at the tree lighting ceremony," Naomi said.

"I'm not sure yet." That was the truth but Leah still felt a stab of emotion. Ben had told her he'd be home early from work to go to the ceremony and reception at the mayor's mansion, but he hadn't officially invited her to go with him and Olivia. She'd already decided that she needed to catch up on the sets that she'd neglected all week when she'd taken over as seamstress. Maybe sanding and painting would keep her mind as busy as her hands and she wouldn't notice that her heart was breaking.

"You need to be there," Naomi said, a secretive smile playing around her lips. "You know that every year the mayor picks a child in foster care to light the tree, right?"

Leah nodded. There was never a dry eye during that part of the ceremony.

"John let it slip the other day who Mayor Morrow is going to choose and I guarantee you'll want to be there."

"We'll see." It was all Leah could say and fortunately Naomi seemed to accept that.

Except for the hum of the furnace, the church was quiet when Leah let herself in later that evening. Just before dinner, Leah had explained to Olivia why she wouldn't be going to the tree lighting with her and although there was flicker of disappointment in Olivia's eyes, she hadn't protested too much. Leah was glad.

She was feeling fragile and didn't know if she would have been able to muster the strength to withstand Olivia's tears.

Ben called late in the day and told her he'd gotten off schedule with a new client and that Rachel would be by to pick up Olivia and he'd meet them there.

Up until that moment, Leah had thought that he'd invite her to go with them but the click of the telephone when he'd hung up had severed that hope.

Lord, I don't know what to do. I thought You brought me here for a reason but now it looks like I'm only making things worse. Ben hardly looks at me and Olivia is sad that he isn't spending as much time at home anymore...what do You want me to do? It's almost Christmas and it might be my first and last Christmas with them. I think Ben is going to let me go. That silly trial period. Why did I ever agree to it?

She knew why. She wanted—needed—to see her daughter. She would have agreed to run barefoot over glass in that moment. She knew with the way she was feeling, she might as well have.

Ben spotted Olivia's cotton-candy-pink hat as soon as he walked onto the grounds of the mayor's mansion. Hundreds of miniature white lights were woven in the wrought-iron fence that surrounded the estate and winked in the trees, creating a Christmas wonderland. There were even tiny flakes of frost shimmering in the air as the temperature dropped. The mansion itself was the perfect backdrop for the festivities, with a candle glowing in every window. Ben had always thought the mansion was rather cold and unwelcoming, but tonight the shadows softened the stern lines of the house and the imposing columns were dressed in garlands of pine and garnished with red velvet bows.

He headed in Olivia's direction. She was bobbing like a cork between Rachel and Eli, who were talking to Zach and Pilar Fletcher, two of their closest friends. Ben had stood up for Eli when he and Rachel had shared a double wedding with Pilar and Zach earlier that fall. As he approached, his gut wrenched with loneliness at the sight of the two couples.

He looked away to grab a moment and ease the knot inside but right in his line of vision were Meg and Jared Kierney, their linked arms another uppercut to his battered emotions. Jared was a reporter for the newspaper but with a twin perched on each shoulder, Ben doubted he was at the ceremony in an official capacity this evening.

"Daddy!" Olivia spotted him and waved.

"Hi, peanut." Ben swung her up into his arms as the two couples shifted their positions to include him in their circle.

"Where's this new nanny that I've heard so much about?" Pilar asked, looking past Ben as if assuming that Leah was close by.

Ben felt everyone's gaze on him.

"She's at church," Olivia said, saving him from the vague response he'd been conjuring. "Painting."

"Tonight?" Eli stared at Ben, a glint in his eyes.

Ben stiffened. "It was her choice."

She would have come with you if you'd asked her.

The words sprouted stubbornly in the cracks that had recently formed in his heart.

"I was hoping we'd get to meet her," Zach put in. "Olivia hasn't stopped talking about her since we got here. She must be pretty devoted to the children's ministry at church if she's giving up this evening for it."

She's devoted to Olivia, but I keep getting in the way.

"How long until the tree lighting?" Ben asked.

Eli glanced at his watch. "About twenty minutes."

He swung Olivia down. "I'll be back."

"You don't have to go back to work, do you, Daddy?" Olivia asked.

The question scraped against him and left him raw. Raw and aware of how his recent inner battles had affected the most important person in his life. "No, I just noticed someone is missing that should be here."

Olivia's eyes widened with hope. "Leah?"

Ben didn't miss the smiles that passed around the small circle of adults, but at the moment he didn't care.

"Leah."

Chapter Fifteen

Leah was just putting the finishing touches on a plywood cutout of a camel when she felt someone's presence in the room. Casting a glance over her shoulder, she saw Ben standing in the doorway, an odd expression on his face.

Just the sight of him pulled at her emotions, as if they were on strings. The paintbrush she'd been holding bounced off her knee and clattered to the floor.

"Let's go."

Leah rose slowly to her feet, helplessly entangled in the pull of his enigmatic gaze. She knew he was talking about the Christmas tree lighting ceremony. She glanced down at her clothes and shook her head. "I'm not dressed for it."

"We have exactly ten minutes and it's going to take at least five to walk to the mansion." His lungs were still burning because he'd left his car parked in the lot and done a marathon dash to the church. Fortunately for his leg muscles, the church and the mayor's mansion were only a block apart.

Leah was still frozen in place and for the first time he noticed her red-rimmed eyes. He knew exactly where to place the blame for that.

You just spread sunshine wherever you go, Cavanaugh.

"Leah, you look great. Olivia is waiting." He pivoted and expected that she'd follow. When he glanced back, she hadn't budged.

"Why?"

"You should be there with us."

He held his breath, hoping it would be enough. Slowly, she nodded.

"I'll help you clean this up later," he promised. "Now we have seven minutes."

"But I…" Leah glanced down at her paint-splattered blue jeans and dabbed her fingers on the fresh spot of yellow that bloomed on her knee.

Ben covered the distance between them in three strides and caught her by the hand. "It's dark, no one will notice."

"It's not dark inside the mansion," she argued as he began tugging her across the room.

"I'll cut the electricity. I know where the box is."

Laughter bubbled out of her, but he felt her resistance give way and she allowed him to tow her up the stairs and outside into the fresh night air.

"Come on," Ben panted in her ear as they jogged down the sidewalk. "I've seen you move faster than this in a full-length wedding gown."

They made it with five minutes to spare. People were

already beginning to file into the mansion to witness the tree lighting, but Ben quickly scanned the crowd and his gaze snagged on Rachel's chestnut hair, which glowed like copper under the lamp light.

"Over there." He realized he was still holding Leah's hand and let go of it just as they stepped into a pool of light.

Leah balked as they reached a small cluster of people, but Olivia burst out of the center and wrapped her arms around Leah's waist.

"This is Leah!"

Leah wanted to slink into the shadows. Both Rachel and the pretty dark-haired woman standing next to her were dressed more appropriately for the occasion, while she was wearing a favorite sweater left over from high school and jeans that could have passed for a paint sample display. As they stared at her, she felt a chunk of hair slip out of its elastic band and land on her shoulder.

"Leah Paxson, this is Zach and Pilar Fletcher," Rachel said.

"Olivia's been telling us all about you," Pilar said with a warm smile.

"And Bear," Zach added.

Leah searched their faces and saw the open friendliness that she'd encountered with Eli and Rachel. No wonder the four of them were good friends.

"You're not wearing a coat, Leah," Pilar noticed. "Aren't you cold?"

"I didn't have time to grab it." She hid a smile as Ben shifted on his feet and looked away. He hadn't even given her time to wash the paint off her hands!

"Here. Take mine." Rachel removed her full-length black wool coat and draped it over Leah's shoulders before she could protest. "I've got Eli to keep me warm."

On cue, Eli's arms went around his wife and he winked at Leah over her head.

Leah cast Rachel a grateful look. Rachel was taller than she was and the coat, which had fallen mid-calf on her, ended at Leah's ankles. It effectively covered up her work clothes, saving her from an acute case of embarrassment. Her kindness made Leah's eyes sting.

"Uh-oh," Zach muttered. "What's going on over there?"

"You're off duty, honey," Pilar said firmly.

Leah followed Zach's gaze to a grove of trees and was surprised to see Mayor Morrow himself almost nose-to-nose with a tall, dark-haired man. It was obvious by the tense posture of both men that they were involved in some sort of confrontation.

For once, Mayor Morrow didn't look like the mild-mannered aristocratic southern gentleman she was used to seeing in the newspaper. Even in the soft lighting, she could see his face was contorted with anger.

"I knew that guy was going to be trouble," Zach said, taking a tentative step forward. Pilar's hand caught his elbow. "It's that investigator, Ross Van Zandt."

"Oh, no you don't. Look, the mayor has his own security people taking care of it."

As they watched, two burly men stepped up and Leah had the uneasy feeling that Mayor Morrow's security, even though dressed respectably in dark suits, were more thuglike than the man in the dark clothes and battered leather jacket.

Leah could almost feel the tension as the stranger squared off with Morrow's security people and then abruptly allowed them to escort him away.

"Are we going in?" Olivia tugged at her arm and she realized that Olivia hadn't even been aware of the drama they'd been watching unfold.

"Cops," Pilar said, but her voice was full of affection as she smiled at her husband. "Never off duty."

They moved toward the mansion and Leah felt another strand of hair disengage and roll off her shoulder. She made a discreet attempt to tug the elastic band off and realized that it was hopelessly tangled. She paused and gave Olivia a gentle push forward.

"You go in. I'll catch up in a second."

Olivia nodded and Leah tried again. Ben paused and turned back. "What's wrong?"

"Nothing." Another tug and she knew she made it worse.

Ben watched her for a second. "Let me help."

"No, really…"

He ignored her and suddenly she felt his fingers in her hair, gently trying to untangle the band from her hair.

Leah couldn't breathe. Their bodies were less than three inches apart and he was close enough for her to inhale the scent of the soap he used, a spicy blend of sandalwood and musk.

Concentrate on something else, Leah.

"There you go." He pressed the elastic band into her hand.

Leah felt her hair tumble down and just as she was about to bolt, Ben's fingers combed through the length of it, calling every nerve ending in her spine to attention.

He's a perfectionist, she reminded herself. *He can't stand things to be out of order...or messy. Even hair.*

She looked up at him to croak out a thank-you and realized that Ben's gaze was focused on her mouth.

He was going to kiss her.

Right on the grounds of the mayor's mansion.

Almost in slow motion, Ben lifted his hand and traced the curve of her face with the pad of his thumb. She could feel the gentle rasp of a callus on his skin....

"Mom. Dad." Olivia was standing several yards away, waving her purple mittens at them like a starter flag. "Come on!"

Ben reacted as if he'd taken a hit to the stomach. He recoiled and pulled away from her.

Leah couldn't move. Olivia had called her *Mom.* And Ben had been about to kiss her. She should have been singing with joy, but the look on Ben's face warned her that the two sweetest things she could ever possibly celebrate weren't a celebration at all.

In fact, they'd probably sealed her termination.

Ben didn't know what he'd been thinking.

Yes, he did. He'd been thinking that Leah's hair felt like satin. He'd been thinking that the curve of her lips would fit against his like they were made just for that purpose. He'd been thinking that she was unique—that her desire to spend time with Olivia overrode any self-consciousness about the way she was dressed or any hurt pride she may have felt knowing that she'd been asked to accompany them at the last minute.

And he'd been thinking that maybe it wasn't just Olivia she wanted to be with.

Then Olivia interrupted them and called her "mom." Just as something inside him nodded at how right that sounded, a wave of pain rose up from the memories he'd carefully guarded and crashed against them. Julia had never heard Olivia call her "mom."

"Look!" Olivia whispered beside him.

Ben realized that the tree ceremony had officially begun and Mayor Morrow was standing next to a fragrant pine that almost grazed the ceiling of the ballroom. In spite of the Italian marble floors and the rich cherry moldings, the Christmas tree was decorated with ornaments that were handmade by local children. That was how the tradition had begun that a child would have the honor of lighting the tree every year.

"Ladies and gentlemen—" Gerald Morrow's voice slid smoothly across the room without the need for a microphone, no evidence of the private tantrum they'd witnessed earlier "—it is our tradition at the mansion to choose a child who is waiting in foster care for a permanent home to light the Christmas tree."

As much as Ben appreciated the gesture, he wondered at the need to announce this every year. It always felt more like an election-time maneuver than a tiding of goodwill.

"This year I've chosen Dylan Taylor."

The kid looked familiar. That's right. He was that miniature juvenile delinquent who'd attacked him with a paintbrush when he'd shown up to help Leah at the church.

Caleb Williams and Anne Smith were standing protectively beside him and Ben noticed that Anne whispered something in the boy's ear. Whatever she said transformed the boy's scowl into a reluctant smile.

Mayor Morrow shook his hand formally and then everyone in the room applauded when Dylan lit the tree.

"I know him from church, Daddy," Olivia whispered. "He's nice to me. He's one of the wise men in the play."

For a moment the ballroom was dark, then the tree sparkled to life, covered in hundreds of multicolored lights that reminded Ben of the stained-glass windows in the church.

"I guess it's over," Ben said, ruffling Olivia's hair. "Let's go."

He needed to put some space between him and Leah.

"But we didn't get any hot chocolate and cookies yet!"

She was killing him. Ben nodded and cut a path through the crowd to the tables of treats like a homing sub. And bumped right into Caleb Williams and Dylan, who'd been granted the privilege to move to the front of the line.

"Hello, Ben, Leah." Caleb leaned down slightly. "And Olivia."

Anne moved into place beside them. "Leah, I was hoping to see you tonight. Kelly Young told Caleb she's in need of some extra hands to wrap gifts this week for the toy drive."

"The more the merrier," Caleb said, looking at Ben.

Great. While he was trying to put distance between

him and Leah, someone was trying to push them together. And this time it wasn't Olivia!

"Sure, I can help," Leah said, careful not to look at him. "But Ben's pretty busy…"

"So far I'm the only guy helping and I don't want to be hopelessly outnumbered," Caleb said good-naturedly. "What do you say, Ben?"

What could he say?

"Sure, no problem. I'll be there."

Chapter Sixteen

So far, Leah still had a job. Every time over the past few days when she felt Ben's gaze on her, she held her breath and waited for him to say the words: *You're fired.*

But he hadn't. And she wasn't sure what was stopping him. Olivia hadn't slipped and called her "mom" again, but it probably didn't matter to Ben. The fact that she'd done it once was enough.

Leah knew she'd never forget the moment she'd heard that word on her daughter's lips. Just like she'd never forget the look in Ben's eyes when he'd leaned down to kiss her.

"And now I have to spend the evening with him and pretend it never happened," she told Bear.

His tail thumped the floor once in sympathy.

The marathon gift-wrapping session for the toy drive was only a few hours away. Even though she'd spent the entire day in a frenzy of decorating and baking in order to surprise Olivia, she still hadn't been able to take her mind off being in the same room with Ben, something they'd carefully avoided since the night of the tree lighting ceremony.

When Leah had tucked Olivia into bed that night, Olivia mentioned that she liked all the lights and wished they had some in their house. Until she'd mentioned it, Leah hadn't realized that the Christmas tree was the only thing in the house that celebrated the upcoming holiday.

When Ben and Olivia had left this morning, she'd searched the closet under the stairs and the basement but couldn't find any more Christmas decorations. Not even a red velvet bow. That's when she'd decided to do some decorating of her own.

She and her mother hadn't had any extra money, but Sara had a gift for taking simple, ordinary things and turning them into something special. Leah liked to think she'd inherited the knack. With one trip to the grocery store, she'd found almost everything she needed.

She emptied a bag of sugar-coated gumdrops into a crystal canister and set it on the coffee table. She tied green and red gingham ribbons around cinnamon sticks and attached them to a rope of garland she'd bought from a man selling them in the parking lot. She filled a hurricane jar with pinecones and cranberries and placed it on the fireplace mantel. She bought a bag of votive candles and decided to show Olivia how to make luminaries to line the sidewalk outside.

But even though her hands were busy, her traitorous thoughts kept drifting back to Ben and the touch of his hand on her face.

"I could just call Anne and tell her that I have a head-ache," she said out loud.

It was true. She could feel tiny currents of pain zig-zagging up the back of her neck. She reached for the phone and paused. Caleb had told them they were short-handed. With a sigh, she slung her miniature backpack over her shoulder and grabbed her car keys. The plan was to pick Olivia up from school and meet at the church to wrap the gifts for the toy drive.

Ben's truck was already parked in the lot when they got there. Olivia had play practice and was met at the front doors by the girls who'd been anxiously watching for her arrival.

Leah walked the short distance to the youth center, which was housed in a separate building.

"Come on, we're just getting started," Anne said at the entrance, motioning her inside. "We have a moun-tain of gifts to wrap."

Leah followed her in and tried to tie off her ragged emotions before she saw Ben. When she followed Anne into the arts-and-crafts room, she was relieved to see that the youth group had taken over, their laughter and energy sending out runners that touched everyone who walked through the door.

Only the top of Ben's head was visible behind a line of plastic construction vehicles.

"Oh, great! Two more hands." A woman wearing a pencil-thin black skirt and matching jacket paused just long enough to smile at Anne and Leah.

"Hi, Kelly. This is Leah Paxson, reporting for duty. She's Olivia Cavanaugh's nanny. Leah, Kelly Young."

"I'm a friend of Ben's," Kelly said with a nod. "I'm sure he's thrilled that you're there. He was having a difficult time finding a replacement for Mrs. Baker."

Oh, yes, he's thrilled, Leah thought.

"We have room at our table." A pretty teenage girl called out to them. She had long blond hair and leaf-green eyes outlined in black kohl. The table in front of her was lined with an entire nursery of baby dolls dressed in white muslin nightgowns. Pilar Fletcher and Rachel were already sitting down, hard at work, while another woman was bent over a tangle of curling ribbon, her face partially concealed by vibrant corkscrew red curls.

"Hi, Leah!" Rachel looked up and smiled. "Pull up a chair and join us."

"At your own risk, mind you." The woman with the red curls tilted her head up, her expression wry. "As you can see, we've already had a slight *incident.*"

"Leah, have you ever met Meg Kierney?" Rachel asked.

"No, but I've seen you at church. You have twins."

"That's my lot in life—to be known as the twins' mother," Meg said with a heavy sigh, although her blue eyes were sparkling with laughter.

"And you wouldn't change it for the world," Pilar put in. "A double blessing, isn't that what it is?"

"I guess I'd have to say a triple blessing." Meg's lips curved into a smile. "You have to take my handsome husband into consideration."

Pilar snorted. "Newlyweds."

"Right, Pilar, as if you weren't staring at your husband like he was the cherry on top of a hot fudge sundae at the tree lighting ceremony the other night. Wasn't she, Leah?"

Leah, who had found an empty chair between two giggling teenage girls, refused to be drawn into the women's lively banter. She didn't know a thing about being a newlywed.

"What I want to know, is this conversation appropriate for young girls?" Anne teased as she joined them.

"In a few weeks, you'll be as dreamy and out of touch with reality as the rest of us newlyweds," Rachel warned her.

Anne's cheeks turned pink and Meg took pity on her. "Okay, more wrapping and less talking or we'll be here until midnight, girls."

"One doll, two pieces of pink tissue paper, a box and then wrapping paper," Pilar said. "We figured out an assembly line. Which one do you want to do, Leah?"

"I'll wrap them in tissue paper."

The girl who'd brought Leah to the table slid a stack of tissue paper down the table to her. "I'm Nikki, by the way. And this is my best friend, Gina."

The two girls were a study in contrasts. Nikki was dressed in a black T-shirt and jeans with a multitude of zippers slashing across the fabric, while Gina wore a conservative khaki skirt and plain white blouse. Her dark hair was pulled back in a braid and the wire-framed glasses she wore gave her a studious look. Unlike Nikki, she wasn't wearing even a hint of makeup.

"I'm Leah."

"You're Olivia's mom, right?" Gina leaned forward. "I see you with her all the time."

Leah hoped Ben hadn't heard the girl's innocent question. "No, I'm her nanny."

"Her nanny!" Nikki echoed the word in surprise. "Wow."

Leah glanced in Ben's direction and wasn't surprised that he'd heard Nikki's exuberant words as they'd bounced around the room. Their eyes met and Leah felt the impact.

"Here, Nikki, you wrap babies, too." Pilar unknowingly came to her rescue. "And Anne, we want to hear all the details about the wedding, right down to the color of the polish you're going to paint your toenails!"

Leah wrapped dolls and listened as Anne began to share the details of her and Caleb's New Year's Eve wedding.

"We're the ones who got them together," Gina whispered to Leah. "We just knew Anne and Pastor Caleb were meant for each other!"

Meant for each other. Leah's head dipped pensively as she mulled over the words.

"Do you have a boyfriend, Leah?" Nikki asked suddenly.

Don't look at Ben! "No."

"We can find you someone," Nikki said blithely, with a fourteen-year-old's confidence that made Leah want to laugh. "We're good at it."

"That's okay." Leah tried to keep a serious expression. "I'm willing to wait on God's timing for a husband." *This time.*

"That's what Anne tells us," Nikki said, her eyebrows dipping in obvious frustration. "Not to rush the whole dating thing."

"She's right." Leah wished she'd had someone who would have explained that to her when she had been Nikki's age. Her mother, who'd been devastated when Leah's father abandoned them and had decided that there was no such thing as a happy ending, hadn't given Leah much guidance in the area of healthy dating relationships. Then Sara had gotten sick…and Leah, vulnerable and scared of losing her mother, had walked right into Jason's arms.

"…it's silver and white with a lot of sparkles."

Leah realized Anne was describing her wedding dress and for a second she thought of the vintage satin gown she'd dropped off at the secondhand store, in spite of Gayle's protests. She'd managed to get the spots of blood out of the sleeve and decided that keeping the dress would only serve as a memory of Ben's cold reminder.

I pay you to take care of Olivia, not me.

The words still had the ability to churn up a rough path through her heart.

Lord, I want to take care of Ben and Olivia. I want to be more than a nanny. I want to be a mother…and a wife.

Ben knew the second Leah walked into the room. It was like he'd suddenly been wired with some kind of internal radar that went crazy when she came into view. He let himself look at her—once—to make sure that she had been accepted into the tightly-knit group of women sitting at the table. Anne, Meg, Pilar and Rachel had been friends for years and sometimes when they were together, caught up in conversation, they forgot everyone else. He relaxed when he heard Leah laughing.

After an hour of sorting through dump trucks and cement mixers and listening to Caleb drone on about his upcoming wedding, Ben decided to check on Olivia. With all the chaos in the room now that the boys in the youth group had shown up, he figured no one would notice if he went AWOL for a few minutes.

Caleb noticed. "Leaving so soon?"

"Just checking on Olivia. Practice must be almost over."

Caleb pushed his fingers through his hair and winced. "I can't believe it. I've been talking about the wedding for an hour, haven't I?"

"An hour and fifteen minutes."

"No kidding." Caleb looked slightly bewildered. "I didn't think I could talk about *anything* for an hour and fifteen minutes."

"That's hard to believe. You're a preacher, aren't you?" Ben couldn't resist.

"I promise if you come back I won't talk about—"

"Raspberry truffle cake, hot versus cold hors d'oeuvres, white roses with baby's breath or ferns." Ben ticked them off on each finger.

"Temporary insanity?" Caleb offered hesitantly.

"I'll give you that." Ben remembered how inept he'd felt at offering suggestions for his own wedding and how much fun he'd had watching Julia make the plans.

Then he remembered a certain young woman sprinting down the sidewalk in front of his house wearing satin and tennis shoes.

Leah, what am I going to do about you?

The night Olivia had called her "mom," he knew he should have asked her to leave. But how could he? He'd almost kissed her. He could still feel the petal-soft warmth of her skin, the silkiness of her hair as it slid between his fingers. The truth was, he couldn't imagine her staying anymore than he could imagine her leaving.

So where did that leave him?

The wave of children pouring out the door to the sanctuary parted around him as he went to find Olivia. She was sitting on the carpeted step in the sanctuary, her arms wrapped around her knees.

"Hey, peanut." He didn't want to go in, but for some strange reason, the sight of the stained-glass windows and the soft satin glow of the woodwork didn't strip the breath out of him this time. He took a few steps inside. "What are you doing?" Briefly, he wondered if someone had hurt her feelings again.

"Just thinking."

Ben hid a smile. "About what?"

"I can't figure something out, that's all. Where's Leah?"

"In the youth center wrapping presents. You know, sometimes good old dad can help you figure things out, too."

"I know, but this…" Olivia paused and Ben sat down beside her. "I was just wondering why God sent Jesus to be born if He knew He was going to die."

Somehow, Olivia had traced the Christmas story to its very heart. Ben struggled to find the answer. "If Jesus hadn't come to earth, we could never be with Him forever."

"It still doesn't make any sense." Olivia looked troubled.

"Because…He loves us. So much that He was willing to die for us."

"Do you believe that?"

Ben knew there was more to the simple question than what Olivia was asking. She was ready to take another step on the journey of faith, but she wanted to know if he was on the same path. Ben found himself wishing that he'd let Olivia take her questions to Leah.

In the past seven years, he hadn't been able to see beyond his battered faith. He'd measured God's love by the blessings in his life, and when Julia died, he'd doubted that love. Now Olivia had forced him to trace his faith back to its source, all the way to a manger in Bethlehem. *For God so loved the world…*

"I believe it." His wobbly faith made its first attempt to stand again.

Olivia's eyes were shining. "I believe it, too."

Leah drove her own car home and met Ben and Olivia in the driveway. It was dark and she could hear Bear's mournful bark as her foot touched the first step.

"I'll take Bear outside," Olivia offered.

Leah turned the light on in the hall and waited to see Olivia's face as she saw the Christmas decorations she'd worked all day to put up.

Bear bounded up to them.

"How did you get out of the laundry room?" Leah scolded.

"He can jump the gate now," Olivia said, wrapping her arms around his furry neck. "I forgot to tell you."

"Well, we knew he was smart," Leah said. "Here's

his leash." With the way Bear was wiggling, she could tell she'd have to wait to show Olivia the decorations.

Ben came in and hung his coat up on the hook, then frowned. "What is this?" He looked at the bottom of his shoe and pulled something sticky off the bottom.

Leah stared at the purple glob and clapped a hand against her mouth. "Oh, no," she moaned, racing into the living room.

The glass canister of gumdrops was on the floor. Empty. There was a half-chewed red bow on the floor and the cinnamon sticks, which had been tasted and rejected, were strewn all over the carpeting. Leah sank to the floor.

Ben surveyed the mess in disbelief. "What happened?"

"I decorated." Leah's words were muffled because her face was buried in her hands.

"Um, maybe next time you should get some ideas from one of those home channels," Ben said.

Was Leah *crying?* Rattled, Ben dropped to his knees and pulled her hands away from her face. Tears raced paths down her cheeks.

"Did you just make a joke?" she demanded.

"I'm sorry."

"No."

"I am," he insisted. "You're upset and I shouldn't have made a joke."

"I wouldn't call it a joke." Leah picked up the remnants of a velvet bow and tossed it at him.

"You wouldn't?"

Leah looked around at the disaster surrounding them. Ben hadn't straightened, picked up or rearranged one thing to re-create his orderly world. He'd been more concerned with her feelings. The thought stoked a warm fire inside her soul.

"I'd call it *progress*."

Chapter Seventeen

"**I**'m nervous."

"It's just a dress rehearsal, sweetie," Leah reminded Olivia as she attached the angel wings to the back of her dress. "The only thing different about today is that everyone is going to be wearing their costumes."

"My throat feels scratchy."

"I'll give you some hot chocolate, that should make the scratchy feeling go away."

A shepherd sidled up to them and he tugged on Leah's sleeve. "I can't find my stick."

"Mrs. Fraser decided not to use the sticks," Leah told him. At the last practice, the shepherds hadn't been able to resist using their shepherd's crooks as swords—against each other—and attempted to turn the Christmas story into a swashbuckling free-for-all. Naomi had wisely disarmed them.

The boy gave her a very unshepherdlike glower and clomped away.

"I can't wait until Christmas," Olivia said, barely able to contain her excitement. "Grammy and Papa are coming back and they'll get to see Bear and…"

"And what?" Leah wound the rope of gold garland into Olivia's hair.

"Nothing." Olivia shivered with excitement but wouldn't tell her.

Suddenly Leah felt a cold spot settle in her stomach. Olivia hadn't mentioned her Christmas wish for a long time and she'd hoped she'd forgotten about it. She should have known better! Olivia's matchmaking attempts had ceased but Leah had a hunch she had another plan in mind.

She tried not to fan the flicker of hope that had been ignited when Ben started coming home for dinner again and spent the evenings in the living room instead of holed up in his office. Once, he'd even asked her if she was going to practice her saxophone.

After Bear had rearranged her Christmas decorations, he'd helped her clean up and the next day he'd come home with several boxes of miniature white lights, which he and Olivia had strung in the bushes outside. Just before Leah went upstairs to get ready for bed, Ben had stopped her.

"I forgot, these are for you, too."

He'd given her a bag of gumdrops.

Progress, indeed. Leah had sent up a silent prayer of thanks. God was at work.

But she still didn't know if Ben was going to let her stay. Olivia was excited for Christmas to come but for the first time, Leah wasn't looking forward to it…not if it meant that her month was officially up and Ben was going to inform her that "it wasn't working" and send her packing.

"Everyone take their places!" Naomi swept into the room wearing a soft pair of blue jeans and a jewel-green sweatshirt. Her red hair was concealed by a baseball cap—a gift from the children—that had the word "Director" printed on it.

"Can we pray that I'm not nervous?" Olivia whispered.

"Sure." Leah stepped closer. "Lord, help Olivia not to be nervous about the play. She's telling a very special story and we ask that the people who watch it next week will be touched and know that You love them."

"And God, help me not get a scratchy throat," Olivia added. "Amen."

Leah hid a smile. "I'm going down to the basement to check the sets one last time and then your dad is going to pick you up from practice and take you home—"

"'Cause you're going Christmas shopping!"

"That's right." Leah bent down and gave Olivia a quick hug. "It's going to take me awhile to find just the right thing for my favorite little girl."

Olivia nodded and skipped away to join the rest of the children who were filing into the sanctuary.

Reverend Fraser had asked them not to move the heaviest part of the set into the sanctuary until after the Sunday morning worship service, so for the dress rehearsal the kids were using just a few of the props they'd painted.

She couldn't believe that everything was finally completed. Naomi had told her that the youth group had been coming in the past few evenings to finish painting and Leah was anxious to see what they'd done.

The light was on in the basement and Leah heard noises coming from the room they'd taken over for props. She expected to see one or two kids inside. She wasn't expecting to see Ben.

"Ben?"

"Hi." He barely glanced at her as began to peel a piece of wood off the side of the stable.

"Ben, don't!"

"I don't know who did this, but they should get their license taken away," he grumbled. "It's off by at least two inches."

"Ben, they don't have licenses because they're kids!" Leah resisted a strong urge to pry the hammer out of his hand and use it to pound some sense into him. "And it doesn't matter if it's off by a few inches. No one will notice."

"I noticed." He reset the board he'd just taken off. "Hand me a nail, please."

"Not a chance. We're not going to touch this stable. It's perfect."

"How can you say it's perfect?" Ben shoved the hammer into his tool belt and grabbed her hand, towing her several yards away. "Look at it! The left side has a space wide enough for an elephant to fit through and the right side wouldn't hold water. The slats in the roof aren't equal. The manger is going to fall off the wall."

She'd hammered the manger into place and a very brave little sheep had volunteered to sit in it to make sure it was sturdy.

"Close your eyes," Leah said.

"Gladly."

She swatted him on the arm. "Ben, close your eyes and picture that night. This stable is probably more true to life than the one you'd come up with. Jesus could have been born in a palace. At the very least, He could have been born in a *house*. But where He was born didn't have to be fancy…or perfect…because *He* is. I'm not going to let you change a thing and hurt those kids' feelings. They gave up their evenings this week to come in and build this thing and that's worth a few gaps and uneven edges."

Leah could tell by the stubborn set of his jaw that she wasn't getting through to him. In fact, he was sliding the hammer out of the loop in his tool belt while she was speaking!

"There's nothing wrong with doing things right." His eyes opened and she saw the pain in them.

They weren't talking about the stable anymore. She took a deep breath and prayed that she'd find the right words.

"No, there isn't, but you have to stop trying to make everything in your life perfect. God can take the most broken, messiest things and make something beautiful and valuable out of them."

"You have no idea what you're talking about. What's happened to you to make you such an expert on what God can do?"

The words landed with the force of a slap and Leah took a step back. "I'm different than the way I used to be."

She couldn't tell him. Not without telling him who

she was. What she was to Olivia. How many times had she asked God to use the things she'd gone through to encourage someone else about His faithfulness? And now, when the opportunity presented itself, she couldn't say a word.

"I tried to do everything right," Ben muttered. "Everything I was supposed to do. Pray. Read my Bible. Go to church. I did it all…and for a while, it worked. Everything went fine. Until Julia…then I thought, what's the use?"

"What's the use?" Leah was overwhelmed by the bitterness that spilled out of him. "Ben, those things aren't a believer's guarantee that nothing bad will ever happen to us, they're to bring us closer to God so that when life gets bad, we *know* He's with us. It's our *relationship* with God that gets us through the hard times. God never promised us an easy, comfortable life, but He did promise that He'll never leave us."

She saw the tears in Ben's eyes before he turned away.

"'My grace is *perfected* in weakness,'" Leah said softly. "That's what God says. His love shines through the cracks in our lives if we let Him in."

He looked like he would break apart if she touched him, but Leah risked it. He'd been keeping all this inside too long. She pried the hammer out of his unresisting fingers and dropped it on the floor, then eased into his arms. For a moment, he stood perfectly still.

She felt the shudder that ripped through him and his arms came around her so tightly that she gasped. For ten minutes they stood together, silently, as Leah absorbed as much of his pain as she could. She didn't know what else to do, but finally the tension in his body eased.

"Thank you," he murmured in her ear.

Now she knew it was between Ben and God. Leah slipped out of the room, leaving the two of them alone.

All the way home, even with Olivia chattering non-stop beside him, Ben tried to process what had just happened in the basement of the church. After Leah had left him alone, he'd sank to the floor and stared at the wooden structure that Leah had assured him was a stable.

He'd missed it. He'd completely missed what his parents had tried to teach him. He'd *acted* like a Christian instead of *being* one and he'd never really gotten to know God at all.

"Are you tired, Dad?" Olivia asked as they arrived home.

She was looking at him and the concern in her brown eyes suddenly reminded him of Leah. "Yup." *Tired of trying to live my life and allowing no room for error.*

What had Leah said? That God's love shines through the cracks in our lives? He'd never looked at flaws quite like that before. For almost eight years, he'd been busily trying to fill the cracks himself, proving that he could do just fine in his own strength. Well, the mortar of pride and self-reliance was crumbling and he'd never felt quite so…free. Not in a long time.

"I'm going to get my pajamas on." Olivia, ever sensitive to the moods around her, planted a kiss on his cheek. Tears stung his eyes. His daughter was a treasure. Leah had been right about that, too—God hadn't left him alone when Julia died. He'd given him Olivia.

Ben went into the living room and flipped on the lights to the Christmas tree. Tinsel brushed against his hand.

God, I really messed up. I've wasted seven years, blaming You for not keeping up Your end of the bargain. I'm sorry...

There was a loud howl from upstairs and Ben leaped to his feet. He met Olivia in the doorway. Tears streamed down her face.

"I broke it!" she wailed. "I broke Leah's donkey."

Ben saw the two pieces of ceramic clenched in Olivia's hand and gently he opened her fingers. One of the donkey's legs had broken off.

"It was an accident, peanut. Leah will understand."

"No." Olivia moaned the word, a fresh overflow of tears rushing down her cheeks. "This is her most special thing, Daddy. I told her I'd take good care of it."

"You know what I think? I think that *you* are more special to Leah than any *thing*," Ben said softly. "I'll fix it and I know she won't be mad at you. Now, go take your bath and when you get out, the donkey is going to look as good as new. I promise."

Olivia sniffled but she carefully transported the pieces into his hands.

Ben found the super glue in with his tools and in no time had reattached the leg. He shook his head. As flawed as the nativity set was, what difference would one tiny crack make? He wondered if Leah had made it when she was a child and that's why it held so much meaning.

He put the donkey back into its place on the dresser and noticed the top drawer wasn't closed all the way. He pushed at it but it didn't close. Opening the drawer, he saw the corner of a picture frame jutting out. That was odd—most people displayed pictures on top of the dresser, not stuck in the drawer.

He glanced down at the photo and smiled. Olivia. Probably taken when she was four or five. The picture looked old, though, and the background didn't look right.

Ben stared at the photo of the little girl and his breath stalled. It wasn't Olivia. Whoever it was, the little girl shared the same soft, caramel-brown hair and wide, impish smile. But her eyes...the exotic amber eyes looking at him were...Leah's.

His hands shook as he put the photo down and picked up several others that had been beneath it. Pictures of Leah as a child.

Oh, God. The plea for strength came from the very center of him. How had he missed it? No wonder people kept mistaking Leah for Olivia's mother.

She was Olivia's mother.

Did she know? Is that why she was here? Had she been stalking his daughter and found a way into their home? Into their lives?

Into their hearts?

"Daddy, did you fix it?"

Ben shoved the photos back into the drawer and closed it. "Go ahead and look, you can't even tell it was broken."

Olivia examined the donkey while Ben concentrated on holding himself together.

"Bedtime." He barely recognized his own voice.

"Are you sure she won't be mad?"

"I'm sure."

He tucked her in and went downstairs, waiting for Leah to return. He ignored Bear's quest for attention as he paced the perimeter of the room, remembering that he'd thought it was silly when people assumed that Leah was Olivia's mother.

Now, who's the fool?

She had to know. He'd told her Olivia's birthday. He'd told her that Olivia had been adopted through Tiny Blessings. And all the time, she'd kept it a secret. Had worked her way into Olivia's heart.

And yours.

He pushed the thought away just as the door opened and Leah came in, carrying several bags. Her cheeks were tinged pink from the cold and he squashed the memory of how, just hours before, she'd held him in her arms while he'd cried out the grief that had been locked inside for years. Now, it was as if he was looking at a stranger.

"Sit down." He kept his voice low, hoping that Olivia had fallen asleep already.

Leah froze in place, her eyes searching his face. And he saw the truth reflected there. Rage poured through him and his fists clenched at his sides.

"What were you planning to do? Abduct her?"

"No!" Leah looked horrified. "You know me better than that."

"I don't know you at all," Ben said coldly. "All I know is that you lied to me from the beginning. Olivia is your daughter, isn't she?"

She didn't even ask him how he knew. "I think so. Yes."

"Leave."

Leah flinched. "Olivia—"

"I'll worry about *my daughter*," he said. "I want you out of this house tonight. Now."

"Ben…I didn't know that Olivia was…I didn't know until I met you that first day. And even then, I wasn't positive."

"But you didn't bother to tell me." Fear and betrayal coursed through him. At anytime, Leah could have simply disappeared with Olivia. It happened all the time. Just as his emotions rose higher, he saw a weary acceptance in the sudden slope of Leah's shoulders and he knew deep inside that that hadn't been her plan. There had to have been another reason why she didn't tell him who she was.

"I should have. I just had to…see her."

She looked so lost that for a split second, Ben wanted to reach out to her. No way. The sin of omission, wasn't that what it was called? "I don't want you to have anything to do with her and if you're planning to go to court, forget it. Everything was legal. I made sure everything was done right."

The words vibrated in the air between them and Leah smiled sadly. "I'm sure you did."

Chapter Eighteen

D ry-eyed, Leah sat in the window seat of her apartment, overlooking the street. It was three o'clock in the morning and she was still dressed, the Christmas gifts she'd bought still in the bags at her feet.

She wished she could cry. Maybe the tremendous pressure in her chest would disappear, but right now the tears had formed a huge, solid block inside and stubbornly refused to move, barely allowed her to breathe.

It was her fault. She should have been honest with Ben from the beginning, but after seven years of wondering about her daughter, it had been like a gift to be able to see her every day. To hear her giggle. To feel her in her arms. A gift she hadn't been able to refuse.

She'd packed her things as quietly as she could but left the nativity set on the dresser for Olivia. What would Ben tell Olivia when she woke up and realized she was gone?

The temptation to sneak in and give Olivia one last

kiss goodbye had been strong and Ben must have known it would be, because he was standing next to Olivia's bed when she eased the door open. With Olivia between them, they stared at each other.

Ben mouthed one word at her. *No.*

Closing her eyes, she could still see the expression on his face. She'd never seen anyone so angry and she knew he had a right to be. She'd come into his home under false pretenses.

God, don't worry about me right now, she begged silently. *Ben was so close to realizing how much he needs You. Don't let anything that I did jeopardize that.*

He must hate her now. And without God, he wouldn't be able to forgive her, either. The knowledge tore at her heart. He said he hadn't known her at all, but now he knew something else about her. She hadn't been perfect. She'd made a decision that had changed the course of her life forever, and even though God had brought his love and forgiveness to dark places in her heart, Ben wouldn't be able to see past the fact that she'd been an unwed teenage mother.

In a day or two, she'd call Mrs. Wallace and ask her if the Andersons had found a replacement for her in England. If they hadn't, maybe they would be willing to hire her again. She couldn't imagine unexpectedly seeing Ben and Olivia again.

"Ben, I'm sorry," Leah whispered as she stared with unseeing eyes out the window.

Two days later, when the doorbell rang, Leah lurched to her feet, wondering if it was Ben.

"Who is it?" Her hands shook as she fumbled with the chain lock.

"Naomi."

Somehow, Naomi had known to come to the apartment instead of the Cavanaughs'. Swallowing hard, Leah opened the door and forced a smile. "Come in."

Naomi swept in, the handle of a basket looped through her arm. "I made this huge batch of chili and decided to share."

With unerring precision, Naomi moved toward the tiny kitchen. She set the basket down on the counter and began to unpack it.

Leah's stomach gurgled in response to the aroma and she prayed Naomi hadn't heard. She hadn't even wanted to go to the grocery store so she'd been surviving on the meager contents of her freezer.

"I made a garden salad because I get so tired of macaroni—the staple of potluck suppers, you know." She winked at Leah.

Leah ventured closer and saw two huge chocolate brownies nestled side by side in a plastic container.

"I have a little time, so I thought I'd join you. If I ate by myself at home, both these brownies would be gone!"

"Ben told you." But if he'd told her, why was Naomi here? With lunch?

"Ben didn't tell me anything," Naomi said gently.

"Then how…"

"Jonah." Naomi studied her for a moment, then appeared to make a decision. "Apparently my son, Mr. Sensitive, told Ben yesterday that he looked like he'd been chewed up and spit out and Ben told him that three nights without sleep will do that to a person. Jonah said that love will, too."

Leah's mouth fell open. "He didn't."

"He did. That's when Ben told him that you were gone. But that's all he would say."

Leah turned blindly away and walked toward the window. "He told me to go. He found out that I'm Olivia's mother. Her birth mother." She expected to hear the door slam, signaling Naomi's departure. Instead, she felt Naomi's arms fold around her.

"It must have been terrible to keep a secret like that."

"I know I should have told him right away, but I knew he'd never hire me and I just wanted a chance to get to know Olivia. By the time I realized…"

"That you were falling in love with Ben?" Naomi finished.

"How did you know?"

Naomi laughed softly. "What is that expression? Been there, done that? I may have children older than you, but I remember what a young woman looks like when she's in love. And believe it or not, I even remember how it feels. Maybe because I wake up every morning and *still* feel it."

The compassion in Naomi's eyes threatened the composure that Leah had been trying so hard to maintain since she'd opened the door.

"I love them both. He didn't even let me say goodbye to Olivia…or give me a chance to explain. He just…told me to leave."

"And he hasn't contacted you since then?"

Leah shook her head. "I talked to Mrs. Wallace and

she didn't know that I was gone. He hasn't even called her yet to find my replacement."

"Maybe he doesn't want to replace you, Leah. Maybe he knows he *can't* replace you."

As much as she wanted to believe what Naomi was hinting at, she knew better. Naomi hadn't seen the look in Ben's eyes that night.

"Ben wouldn't want someone like me. He doesn't believe in mistakes. Everything has to be right. I didn't do things right, Naomi. Before I came to know the Lord, I got involved with a boy who made me all kinds of promises that I believed. But I didn't give Olivia up for adoption so I could go on with my life, I needed to know that *she* would have a life. A life with a mom and dad who loved her. Ben told me once that he hoped Olivia wouldn't search for her birth mother some day because he doesn't know what kind of person she is."

"I know what kind of person she is," Naomi said. "The kind of person that I'm blessed to have as a friend. And the man who loves you, Leah, won't hold your past against you. He'll only see it as a testimony to God's grace and faithfulness."

"I think that all Ben sees is a person who wasn't honest with him."

"Then let's pray that God opens his eyes, shall we?"

Naomi led her to the futon and they sat together, hands clasped.

"Lord God, we don't know the future but we trust that You do, and everything that happens to us has to filter through Your loving hands first. Give Leah Your peace about this situation and let her rest in the knowl-edge that Your plans for her bring hope, not harm."

As soon as Leah heard the words, it was like a flood lamp suddenly switched on inside her. The past two days had been one long nightmare because she hadn't re-membered to claim God's promise. *A hope and a future.*

She hugged Naomi, who she knew God had sent as a reminder of His love. Just like He'd brought Rebecca into her life five years ago. And knowing she hadn't been taking care of herself, He'd even provided lunch!

Despite Leah's protests, Naomi insisted on serving them and brought the bowls of chili over to the coffee table. Leah hadn't eaten since the previous afternoon and she tried not to throw good manners out the win-dow as she took a small bite.

"You are going to watch Olivia in the Christmas Eve program, aren't you?" Naomi asked.

Leah was silent. That was another question that she had been agonizing over the past few days. She had no idea what Ben had told Olivia about the reason why she'd left, but he'd made it clear when he wouldn't let her say goodbye that he didn't want her near Olivia.

"I don't know what to do. I'm afraid of how Olivia will react if she sees me. I'm afraid what Ben will do." Leah shifted restlessly. "But I want to see her, Naomi. More than anything. She's been a little nervous about the solo she's going to sing…."

"Then you need to be there. The last time I checked, there wasn't a list posted on the doors of the church that said who can, and can't, attend the services there!"

"But Ben…" Leah caught her bottom lip in her teeth.

"I don't want to make things difficult for him, or cause a rift between him and Olivia."

"Then we'll just have to be creative, won't we?"

"Creative?"

"Creative." Naomi nodded thoughtfully. "For instance, did you know that the alcove in the balcony has a terrific view of the sanctuary?"

"I thought the balcony was sectioned off."

Naomi's vivid blue eyes sparkled. "I have connections."

Chapter Nineteen

"Is Leah going to be at the Christmas program tonight?"

Olivia's quiet words tugged at Ben and he flipped over the pancake he was making for her breakfast.

"I don't know."

"But Daddy..."

"I don't know," Ben repeated, then felt guilt singe the already tattered edges of his heart when he saw the expression on her face.

"She said she was going to get me a confidence outfit." Olivia trailed her fork through the puddle of syrup on her plate, her brown eyes forlorn.

"A what?" Ben stared at the pancake he'd just made. It wasn't a normal, everyday pancake. It was a golden-brown caterpillar. What had Leah done to him?

"Leah says that God always make us feel good on the inside, but sometimes a girl needs to feel good on the outside, too, so her inside and her outside matches. She said when she talked to you about taking care of me, she was wearing her confidence outfit because she was nervous."

Now he remembered—her confidence outfit. Most women would have gone for sensible navy or basic black. Well, maybe black combat boots counted....

She hadn't looked nervous that morning. She'd gently teased him, called him Mr. Banks after the stuffy, no-nonsense character in *Mary Poppins*. And she'd looked at the picture of Olivia without a change in expression, even though she must have known she was staring at a picture of her own child. And although he'd missed it, half the population of Chestnut Grove had noticed the resemblance between them!

He still couldn't believe that all this time, Olivia's birth mother had been living with them. As the shock had begun to wear off, his initial anger had faded, too. The house was incredibly empty without Leah. Even Bear shuffled around the place, looking lost.

I know just how you feel, buddy, Ben had told him the night before. He hadn't even called Mrs. Wallace to find a replacement for her. The past two days, he'd rearranged his schedule to pick Olivia up after school and then drop her off at the Noble Foundation, where Rachel kept an eye on her for an hour. He knew that she'd need someone to take care of her during the Christmas holiday, but so far he hadn't been able to pick up the phone to start the process.

"I guess I don't need a confidence outfit." Olivia pushed her plate away and Ben noticed that she'd hardly touched her breakfast. "Daddy, do you think Leah is going to stop being mad at me pretty soon?"

"Mad at you?"

"For breaking her donkey." Tears welled up in Olivia's eyes.

Ben dropped the spatula, sending a spray of pancake batter down the length of his jeans. No wonder over the past few days his normally cheerful, bubbly daughter had slowly deflated into a quiet, somber stranger. She hadn't believed his vague explanation of a family emergency for Leah's absence; she thought she was to blame.

"Leah isn't mad at you."

"Then why won't she come back? She promised to sit in the front row when I sing my solo…and I prayed and prayed last night that she'd come back so I could tell her I'm sorry. And she didn't."

Olivia didn't need to ask for Leah's forgiveness—he did. He hadn't known how much light she'd brought into his life until he realized how dark it was now that she was gone. Somehow in the past month, a petite, tawny-haired whirlwind had managed to overturn his controlled, well-ordered world…and he didn't miss that world a bit.

God, what am I supposed to do? I didn't expect this. I didn't expect to fall in love again. I didn't expect Leah.

And he didn't expect he'd be turning to the God he'd walked away from for strength, but that's exactly what he was doing. And he had Leah to thank for that, too.

He was beginning to realize that he had Leah to thank for a lot of things.

"Get dressed. We're going out."

"Are we going to find Leah?"

Not quite yet. He'd been blinded that night by anger,

by the fact that she hadn't told him the truth. Remembering her stricken face at the cold way he'd treated her—just hours after she'd reached out to him—he sent up a silent prayer that she would forgive him. Even though he didn't deserve it.

"We're going shopping for a confidence outfit."

Olivia shrugged. "I don't need one."

"That's okay." Ben pulled Olivia into his arms and gave her a fierce hug. "I do."

"I've heard of bats in the belfry..."

Leah heard the whispered words behind her and jumped. Twisting around, the shadows were illuminated by Jonah Fraser's killer smile.

"Shh." Leah glanced around. Even though she'd come an hour before the Christmas Eve program, the church was already filling with eager parents armed with cameras and camcorders. "How did you know I was up here?"

Jonah's lips twitched. "My mother missed her calling. She should have been CIA. She told me you were up here in the balcony and that I should invite you over to our house after the service. We have a very sacred Christmas Eve tradition of watching *It's a Wonderful Life* and eating way too much fudge."

"I don't want to intrude on your family."

"I hate to remind you, but you're family, too," Jonah pointed out. "Sisters and brothers in Christ, you know."

Leah considered what was waiting for her at her apartment—leftover chili from her impromptu lunch with Naomi. No Christmas tree. No decorations. No one to laugh with, or share stories with. No Ben and Olivia. "Thank you, I'd love to come."

Jonah smiled his approval and Leah wondered how any woman could remain immune from his rugged charm. Any woman except her, she amended silently. Her heart belonged completely to a handsome, stubborn carpenter.

"Great. Now, I better help corral those restless sheep down there or we'll have a stampede," he drawled, tipping an imaginary hat at Leah before he sauntered away.

Leah felt her heart lift slightly. Sisters and brothers in Christ. A reminder that she wasn't alone. That she did have a family.

Thank You, she murmured, closing her eyes.

When she opened them, Ben and Olivia were standing below her in the doorway. Olivia was already wearing her angel costume and a halo of gold garland encircled her head with her hair carefully curled around it.

Who had fixed her hair?

Leah felt a rush of despair course through her. All the evenings that she'd brushed out Olivia's hair while they'd sat on the bed and talked came rushing back. Over the past week, she'd wondered whether the time she'd had with Ben and Olivia was worth the pain she was feeling now. There was a one-way plane ticket to England waiting for her at the airport for New Year's Eve. Mrs. Wallace had called her that morning to tell her that the Anderson family wanted her back.

She saw Ben look around the church, his gaze slowly moving over the pews, and she took a step back into the shadows. As usual, her heart had jumped out of its normal rhythm like a runaway train at the sight of him. He'd traded in his casual clothes for black wool pants and a heather gray dress shirt, complete with a silver-and-black tie. He looked like he'd stepped off the pages of a popular men's magazine, which reminded her that she didn't even have photos of him and Olivia to remember them by.

As if you'd forget, she chided herself, knowing she'd lovingly memorized every detail about them, from the way Olivia scrunched up her nose when she labored over her spelling words to the way the corner of Ben's lips lifted slightly when his wry sense of humor surfaced.

Heart aching, Leah watched Olivia give Ben one last hug before she went to join the other children waiting for the program to begin.

Every time a group of people filed past him, looking for a place to sit, Ben scanned their faces. There was no sign of Leah anywhere. He couldn't believe she wouldn't come to church on Christmas Eve to watch Olivia sing her solo in the play. For the first time, he felt a trickle of fear.

Where was she?

She was missing everything. The sets she'd so painstakingly worked on, the costumes she'd patiently sewn in the evenings…and Olivia. And he had only himself to blame.

"I'm scared. Can we pray, Daddy?" Olivia had tugged on his hand just before Naomi Fraser had hurried her away.

It was the first time he'd ever prayed with his daughter and promised himself that it wouldn't be the last. Olivia's faith was already bearing fruit—she knew exactly who to turn to when she was afraid. He may have messed that up before, but hopefully he was wiser now.

I'm scared, too, Lord, he admitted silently. *Scared that Leah won't believe that I love her. Scared that she won't forgive me for telling her to leave...for believing that she would do anything that would hurt Olivia.*

Ben realized that all the children had appeared up front and Olivia was standing on a footstool above the shepherds, a tiny cluster of angels behind her. She sought him out and Ben gave her a thumbs-up sign that only slightly erased the anxious look on her face. Then, he saw her look carefully around the room and he knew exactly who she was looking for.

Reverend Fraser stepped into view and opened the program with prayer, then Ben watched as Mary and Joseph began their weary journey up the center aisle to the stable. He heard a low ripple of laughter spread through the congregation and as the children passed him, he realized why. Joseph was gently patting "Mary" on the back as she wobbled from the weight of the lumpy pillow under her robe. The girl was one of the girls from Caleb's youth group—Gina, if he remembered her name correctly. He was sitting at the end of the pew when she suddenly glanced at him, her eyes wide and troubled. And very young.

Ben's heart took a sudden dive into his polished shoes. Leah must have been sixteen when she'd learned she was pregnant with Olivia—not much older than the girl who was playing the part of Mary. Had anyone supported her during those nine months? Leah had mentioned her mother dying after a long illness, but he realized he knew very little about her past. Who had been there for her? Who had patted her back and encouraged her along the way?

Leah had taken a risk to meet the child she'd given up for adoption. And he was planning to take one, too, wasn't he? Deciding to locate his own birth mother?

I'm sorry, Leah. If I were you, I would have done the same thing.

As Mary and Joseph passed him, Ben looked for Leah once more but now the lights had dimmed. All he could see were the children in the front. Olivia's turn came and he heard her words ring clearly through the church.

"Do not be afraid. I bring you good news of great joy that will be for all people...."

Naomi sat at the piano and as she started to play, soft music swept through the sanctuary. Olivia's voice never wavered as she sang the first two verses of "O Holy Night." When she finished, there was a spontaneous burst of applause from everyone in the church.

Olivia ducked her head and Ben saw Leah reflected in the slightly mischievous smile that flashed across her face. She was there and gone in a fraction of a second.

"That's your daughter, isn't it?" The woman sitting next to him waved her program to get his attention.

Ben nodded. "Olivia."

"I love her costume," she whispered. "Where did you find it?"

"Her mother made it."

* * *

After the program ended, Olivia rushed up to him, halo askew. Ben knew what she was going to ask before she even opened her mouth to speak. "Did you see Leah?"

He pulled her against him. "No, peanut, I didn't."

Olivia's eyes immediately filled with tears. "Why?"

Because you were an idiot? Because you let your pride take control and wouldn't let Leah explain? Take your pick, Cavanaugh!

"Why don't we stop by her apartment before we head for home?" Ben suggested, praying that Leah was still in Chestnut Grove.

Olivia's expression was still doubtful, as if she, too, was beginning to wonder if Leah was ever going to be part of their lives again.

It took them at least fifteen minutes to weave through the crowds of people that lingered to talk, and just as they reached the door, Ben found himself face-to-face with Reverend Fraser.

"Ben. It's good to see you here." John Fraser's booming voice cut through the chatter and he extended his hand. For the first time in a long time, Ben didn't try to avoid him or suffer through his well-meaning but misguided attention.

"It's good to be back," Ben said. And it was the truth. Sitting through the Christmas program, he realized that he'd forgotten the feeling of belonging he'd had when he'd attended worship services. After Julia's death, he'd turned away from the people who had tried to reach out to him. He'd rebuffed their attempts to encourage him, and in the process, had drifted even further away from the Lord.

Reverend Fraser's attention moved to Olivia. "Your solo was beautiful, Olivia."

"Thank you," Olivia murmured politely.

Reverend Fraser frowned slightly and glanced at Ben. "Is something wrong?"

"We lost Leah," Olivia said, so dismally that Reverend Fraser's lips twitched.

"Leah Paxson?"

"She was supposed to be here tonight. She *promised*."

Ben pulled Olivia's braid lightly. "We'll find her. Uh, you didn't happen to see her tonight, did you, Reverend Fraser?"

Reverend Fraser hesitated just long enough to give Ben hope, but then he shook his head slowly. "I haven't seen her, but you'd have to ask my wife about that."

She had been there. Ben could see it in his eyes. He wasn't lying, but Ben knew there was more than he was able to share.

"We'll see you in the morning, Reverend Fraser." He grabbed Olivia's hand and started for the doors. If Leah had been there, she was probably back to her apartment by now.

Olivia could barely contain her excitement as they drove down Main Street. When they turned down Leah's street, lights winked everywhere…except in her apartment. It was completely dark. There wasn't even the soft glow of a night-light to signal that she'd be returning anytime soon.

He and Olivia stared up at the window.

"I don't think she's there," Olivia said in a small voice, threaded with hope. "Do you think she went home?"

Home. Ben knew she meant their house, which was exactly where Leah should be. Sitting on the couch next to that tinsel-laden tree with Bear at her feet. He'd been so sure that she'd be at the Christmas Eve service... Ben stared up at the darkened apartment, feeling totally helpless. If Olivia wasn't with him, he'd spend the entire night in his truck, waiting for Leah to come back.

"We'll come back tomorrow," Ben said.

"I have to give her the present I made for her."

He remembered the large, gold-wrapped package that he'd put under the tree that morning. "So do I."

Chapter Twenty

Leah's alarm clock went off on Christmas morning to the soft strains of "O Holy Night." Closing her eyes again, she imagined Olivia standing in front of the entire congregation, singing the first verses.

It had taken every ounce of self-control she had not to rush down from the balcony and tell Olivia that she'd kept her promise. She was there to watch her first solo.

Then she'd look at Ben. It was obvious he was afraid that she was going to show up. He was constantly glancing over his shoulder or watching the entrance. Once, she even saw his gaze move upward, toward the balcony, but she moved closer to the pillar and knew he couldn't possibly see her.

She'd gotten back to her apartment at midnight, having spent a boisterous evening with the Fraser clan. At first she felt uncomfortable, but Ruth and Dinah, John and Naomi's daughters, quickly made her feel at home. Jonah had only given her half the information in his as-

sessment of Christmas Eve at the Fraser household—
they did eat too much fudge, but they also had to *make*
it first. And making it, Leah discovered, was actually
more fun than eating it, especially with Ruth seizing
every opportunity to sabotage Jonah's candy-making
attempts.

Naomi had wrapped a quilt around her shoulders
while they watched *It's a Wonderful Life,* but Leah
found it difficult to focus her attention on the movie because she couldn't stop imagining what Ben and Olivia
were doing.

Both Naomi and John had encouraged her to spend
the night in their guest bedroom, but Leah couldn't. She
had a mission to accomplish early in the morning and
she didn't want to disturb anyone.

It was her *mission* that pushed her out of bed at five-
thirty on Christmas morning. She had several hours before the Christmas day service started at church and so
she pulled on a faded pair of blue jeans and a black
hooded sweatshirt, then pulled on her favorite boots.

Her heart pounded in response to the huge risk she
knew she was taking by going to Ben's, but she had to
let Olivia know that she hadn't forgotten about her.
Tucking the brightly wrapped present under one arm,
she slipped out of her apartment.

Ben decided that if he strung together the actual minutes that he'd slept that night, it would probably equal
a whopping ten. He finally gave up and went downstairs,
where fortunately the coffeepot had been programmed
for a five o'clock feeding. Bleary-eyed, he poured him-

self a cup of coffee and leaned against the counter, closing his eyes.

Lord, please help me out here. I have no idea how to reach Leah. You sent her to us and I was the one who told her to leave…I messed up…

Bear whined at the front door.

Olivia was still sleeping so Ben anchored his coffee cup in his hand and went to let him out. Bear's tail was wagging so hard that his ears were shaking and Ben chuckled as he reached down.

"Merry Christmas to you, too, you big…" He pulled open the door and almost tripped over Leah, who was kneeling on the front step, her mittened hands clutching a Christmas present wrapped in pink with a frothy silver bow.

She jumped to her feet and almost lost her balance as Bear tried to lick her face.

For a moment they just stared at each other. Ben couldn't believe she was actually—finally—within reach. *Thank You, God.*

"I…" Leah backed down a step and wouldn't look at him. "This is for Olivia."

"Leah…" She was halfway down the front walk before he found his voice.

She ignored him.

"Leah…I need to ask you something…about Olivia," he called, even as his mind scattered in different directions to search for a question that would keep her with him.

She stopped and turned around, waiting, but her slender shoulders were rigid, as if one misspoken word would carry her out of his life forever.

"Will you come inside for a minute?" He held the door open for her.

She took a few tentative steps forward and when she brushed past him, the soft scent of vanilla tantalized him. As Ben started to close the door, Bear peered forlornly at him on the other side.

"Just work with me, okay, buddy?" he whispered. "I'll let you back inside in a few minutes."

Leah was standing several yards away and Ben motioned toward the living room. "In there."

He'd lit the tree and the lights glowed softly, reflecting off the tinsel and the glass ornaments. He wondered if Leah would notice that they'd put her nativity set on the coffee table.

"I got these for Olivia and I need your opinion," he said, feeling the weight of Leah's silence right down to the bone. It was the one present he hadn't had time to wrap because he'd had to smuggle them out of Olivia's sight while they shopped for confidence outfits. He pulled a box out from behind the tree and walked over to her. "What do you think? Are they like yours? I couldn't remember."

It was killing him to be so close to her and not touch her.

She looked in the box and he saw the shadow of a smile come and go. "She'll love them," Leah said quietly.

"Are they like yours?"

Leah glanced down at her feet and then at the boots nestled in tissue paper. "They're close." She eased away from him and before he could blink, she was moving toward the door.

"What about her second wish?"

Leah kept going.

"Olivia had two wishes, you know."

Was he *trying* to torture her, Leah wondered, barely able to see because of the tears that blurred her vision. She knew she shouldn't have come to the house, but she'd never imagined that Ben would be up before six o'clock in the morning. He was dressed in faded blue jeans and a soft denim work shirt, his jaw shadowed with stubble, and all she'd wanted to do when she saw him was launch herself into his arms and stay there until she was old and gray.

"Leah, don't leave."

Now she was hearing things. Ben couldn't have possibly said those words.

"Please."

Leah turned around. Ben was still standing in the exact same spot he'd been a minute ago, but now she looked at his face for the first time. And what she saw in his eyes...

"If you walk out that door, Olivia and I won't get our Christmas wish," Ben said, walking toward her.

Leah moved away from him. "You don't mean that."

Seeing the shattered expression on her face, Ben was painfully aware that he was reaping the consequences of the seeds he'd sown in anger. How would he ever convince her now that they were meant to be together, meant to be a family?

"I know I should have let you explain the night I found those pictures and I'm sorry. You'd never do anything to hurt Olivia. You love her."

"It was wrong not to tell you the truth. All I could see was that God had given me a chance to know my daughter and I didn't let myself think about anything else. I guess I started pretending, just like Olivia, that I fit in here and that we were supposed to be together."

"You *do* fit." He couldn't imagine life without her and he couldn't risk her walking out the door. "I love you, Leah. I wanted to tell you last night but you weren't at the play…and then you weren't home. But I promised myself that if it took all day today to find you, I would."

For a split second, he saw some emotion flare in her eyes but then it was gone. There was still a barrier between them that he had no clue how to breach.

Her arms were wrapped protectively around her middle and she shook her head. "You don't know anything about me."

Suddenly it was as if God Himself bent down and whispered something in his ear. As if he'd been given a chance to glimpse Leah's heart, he knew what was preventing her from accepting his love. "I know everything I need to," he said. "Because of you, I found my faith again. I know how to make caterpillar pancakes. I can't read now unless there's a saxophone playing in the background. Leah, you make my heart bigger. Don't take that away."

A ragged breath tore through her and Ben couldn't wait another second. In two strides he covered the distance between them and pulled her against him. "It's in the past," he murmured. "And some wise person told me that the cracks in our life let God's light shine through. Now, please put me out of my misery and tell me—"

"I love you, too," Leah said, and felt Ben's arms tighten around her.

"If I start kissing you now, I have this feeling that I'm not going to be able to stop," Ben murmured, but then, as if he couldn't help it, he brushed a lingering kiss on her lips. "Let's go wake up Olivia. It's time for her to open her gifts, although, I think you may be hard to wrap."

"Ben!" Leah laughed and reluctantly moved out of the comfort of his arms. He loved her. The truth was in his eyes and it both amazed and humbled her.

"Leah?" Olivia was standing in the doorway, her hair mussed from sleep but her eyes wide.

"You did ask for a mom for Christmas, didn't you?" Ben said with a casual shrug that belied the laughter in his eyes. "Wasn't this the one you had in mind?"

In a heartbeat, Olivia had bolted across the room and jumped into Leah's arms. "Are you staying?" She whispered the words in Leah's ear, clinging to her.

Leah managed a nod. She felt Ben's hands on her shoulders, his touch warm and loving. She couldn't answer Olivia's question, so Ben did.

"She's staying."

A sharp bark outside the window caught their attention and Ben laughed. "He's reminding us that we're missing someone."

"Then let's open presents!" Olivia said excitedly. "Bear gets one, too. Daddy bought him a rubber hamburger."

"It probably should have been a tire," Ben grumbled, but Leah knew better. Bear was family.

Leah sat on the floor and pulled Olivia into her lap,

content to cuddle her and breathe in the faint scent of strawberry shampoo.

"Open this one first, it's from me," Olivia said when Ben returned with Bear in tow.

Leah carefully peeled off the bow and pulled off the paper, revealing a miniature wooden stable, the perfect size for her nativity set. There were uneven pieces of wood and globs of dried carpenter's glue in the seams. And Leah loved it.

"Daddy cut the wood and I put it together."

"It's perfect." Leah snuggled her closer.

"And this one is from me," Ben said, pulling a large box out from under the tree.

Leah, still overwhelmed, tried to smile. She pulled open the flaps and looked inside. A leather bound photo album was nested in bright red tissue paper.

"I doubt it will take us long to fill that up," Ben said softly, his eyes promising a new beginning for all of them.

"I think there's something else in there." Olivia leaned forward and poked at the box.

Leah moved the tissue paper and she caught a glimpse of lace. Heart in her throat, she hesitated.

"Technically, the dress is from Gayle at the second-hand store," Ben said as Leah carefully pulled the wedding gown out of the box. "But I know women like to… what's the word…accessorize." He winked at Olivia. "I'll provide the jewelry that goes with it."

"Ben…" Was he asking her to *marry* him?

"I've been carrying this around with me for two days," Ben said, pulling a small velvet box out of the pocket of his jeans. He looked at Olivia. "You're the official witness. Olivia's Christmas wish was for a mom but I'm afraid you have to make *my* wish come true first. Will you marry me, Leah?"

She had to be dreaming.

"Say yes!" Olivia nudged her.

"Yes." Leah's fingers shook as Ben slid an exquisite ring on her finger, a scattering of tiny diamonds winking from the three strands of gold that were woven together.

"I bought it at an antique store," Ben said softly. "It's not new, but it's…"

"Perfect." Olivia and Leah said the word at the exact same time, then they fell together, laughing.

"Now you'll be my mommy for real," Olivia said. "I won't have to pretend anymore."

Later, when Olivia had taken Bear outside to play, Ben pulled Leah gently into the shelter of his arms. "When should we tell her the truth?"

"Are you sure?"

Leah smiled. "We can wait until the right time. I'm not going anywhere."

Ben brushed his face against her hair. "You've got that right."

"Merry Christmas!"

The greetings rang through the church as Ben ushered Leah and Olivia through the wide front doors of the church. Eli and Rachel motioned to them and made room in their pew. Eli couldn't quite hide his surprise and Ben grinned at him as he sat down.

"Is this an opportunity for me to say I told you so?" Eli asked, tossing a meaningful look at Leah, who was all smiles beside him. "Because I really hate to let those slip by. Especially when it comes to my older brother."

"Go ahead then," Ben sighed. "Get it over with."

"I told—"

Suddenly, Rachel let out a little shriek and Eli frowned as the two women embraced. Then comprehension dawned in his eyes.

"Okay, I'm still waiting for the 'I told you so.'"

"I'll save that for tomorrow, right now I think I'll just say congratulations…and that it looks like my brother finally came to his senses." He lowered his voice. "So when is the wedding?"

"Today. Tomorrow. As soon as we can arrange it." Ben wasn't going to be without Leah a second longer than he absolutely had to.

"Uncle Eli, look at my boots. They're just like Leah's!" Olivia lifted her foot and Eli's eyebrows rose. With a laugh, Leah lifted the hem of her velvet dress so the black leather was visible for a moment.

"I'll be praying for you with that pair," Eli muttered.

"What can I say, like mother, like daughter."

Their eyes met and Eli sucked in his breath. "I think I might have missed something here."

"Not this time, but try to keep up, *little brother.*"

After the service, news of their engagement traveled through the congregation and Ben couldn't take two steps forward without someone stopping him and Leah to offer their congratulations.

When Zach Fletcher paused to shake his hand, he ignored the knowing look on the detective's face. "Eli already beat you to it, so you may as well save your breath."

"I don't know what you're talking about, Cavanaugh," Zach said good-naturedly. "All I was going to say was Merry Christmas…and congratulations."

"Sure you were."

Zach laughed and moved on to shake Reverend Fraser's hand.

"We better get going. Mom and Dad are probably pulling into the driveway while we speak." Eli put his arm around Rachel's shoulders. "We'll see you there. You probably want to stop at home first."

Ben pretended to consider the question and drew Leah against him. "What do you think, Leah? *Home* first?" He murmured in her ear.

The answer was reflected in her smile. "Home sounds good to me."

Chapter Twenty-One

"**S**top fidgeting, Anne, you look beautiful!"

Anne Smith, soon-to-be Anne Williams, dutifully stood still as Meg fussed with the train of her wedding gown.

"Caleb is going to fall over at the sight of you," Pilar said, snapping another picture.

Leah watched with a smile as Anne turned slightly in front of the mirror and the movement sent the white-and-silver gown billowing out around her. With her blond hair carefully curled and a tiara holding her veil in place, Leah thought that she looked like she'd just stepped out of the pages of a fairy tale.

For some reason, Rachel had called her the night before at her apartment and asked her if she'd like to come to the church early and help them get Anne ready.

"You know, makeup, giggling, all that girlie kind of stuff," Rachel had said.

Even though Rachel had been nice to her on the few occasions they'd met, Leah felt the warmth of her friendship in a new way since she and Ben had announced their engagement. And any fears she'd had about being accepted by Peggy and Tyrone had been put to rest the minute they'd walked into Eli and Rachel's home after the service on Christmas morning. Both Ben's parents had embraced her like a long-lost daughter and even during a quiet lull in the day when the four of them were alone and Ben told them who Leah was, the loving look in Peggy's eyes had remained while Tyrone had coughed a bit self-consciously.

"God works it all out. Never doubted it for a minute," he'd said, clapping his hand on Leah's shoulder. "Welcome to our family, Leah."

"Everyone in the picture!" Pilar directed, tugging Leah back to the moment. "You, too, Leah. Quit trying to hide!"

"In a few hours, when the clock strikes midnight, you won't be Cinderella anymore," Meg teased. "You'll be Mrs. Caleb Williams."

Anne blushed. "We thought New Year's Eve would be a good time to celebrate a new beginning."

The door opened and Naomi poked her head in. "Are you ready, Anne?"

Meg poked her in the ribs. "Breathe!"

"I'm ready," Anne gasped.

Leah hurried to join Ben and Olivia in the sanctuary and when she slid into the pew, Ben put his arm around her.

"I know it's wrong, but I'm jealous," he murmured.

"Jealous?"

"I want us to be the ones getting married tonight."

Leah felt her cheeks heat up. "Then I'm jealous, too."

The music changed and the men filed to the front of the church.

"It's the delinquent," Ben whispered.

Leah chuckled. "Dylan is a great kid. Honestly, one attack with washable paint isn't the beginning of a life of crime. He happens to be the best man."

"If you say so."

Leah saw the teasing glint in his eyes and grinned. This was a side to Ben that was brand-new and she loved it. He was still serious but now he seemed...*relaxed*. Content. Leah thought at first that it was as if the Lord had peeled away his bitterness and revealed the man that Ben had been. But then she began to realize that it was more than that. She was starting to see glimpses of the man that Ben was *becoming*, too.

The ceremony was beautiful and Leah found herself sniffling through the entire thing.

"You may kiss your bride." Reverend Fraser stepped away from the couple and Caleb took Anne into his arms. There was a rousing cheer from the congregation.

"This is the part in the ceremony where I would traditionally present the bride and groom to you, but Caleb and Anne asked me before we began if we could do things a bit differently. It seems that instead of walking down the aisle together—the two of them—they'd like to include someone else this evening." Reverend Fraser choked up a bit. "Dylan, Caleb and Anne would like you to accompany them. It seems that we have more than the blessing of a couple today, we have the blessing of a *family*. The adoption is going to go through and Dylan will officially be Anne and Caleb's son."

"Tissue?" Leah squeaked to Ben as applause threatened to shake the stained-glass windows.

"No way," Ben said. "I need it."

"Come on you guys, it's time for the bride to toss the bouquet!" Gina and Nikki appeared at the table and Olivia jumped up excitedly.

"Come on, Leah!" Olivia tugged on her arm.

"That's for single girls," Leah protested.

"You're only engaged," Nikki shrugged. "Technically you're still single."

Leah looked helplessly at Ben, who gave her a mock glower and repeated one of Olivia's favorite lines. "I don't like *technically*."

"Since when?" Leah teased, rising to her feet as the three girls clung to her.

Five minutes later, a dazed Leah returned to the table, holding the bouquet. She slid in to the chair next to Ben.

"It was rigged," she said decisively. "I know it."

"Doesn't that mean you're the next one to get married, Miss Paxson?"

"Yes, I believe it does, *Mr. Cavanaugh.*"

"All this sweetness is making me hungry for cake," Meg said loudly from the end of the table.

"What kind would you like?" Jared asked. "White or chocolate or raspberry?"

Meg smiled brightly. "Yes."

Jared tossed an apologetic look at Ben and Leah. "Do you want pickles to go with that?" he said under his breath, not realizing that at that exact moment there would be a lull in conversation.

Everyone stared at them.

Meg's face turned as red as her hair. "Jared!"

"Sorry." Jared didn't look a bit sorry, he looked proud. And excited.

"I'm jealous again," Ben muttered.

"Me, too."

Olivia plunked down in her father's lap. "Do you want to know my Christmas wish for next year?"

Ben tickled her. "No."

"A brother. Or a sister. Or maybe both." Olivia's eyes were sparkling with mischief.

"Go get cake," Ben ordered.

Giggling, Olivia slipped off his lap and disappeared into the crowd.

"Both?" Ben repeated, looking a bit dazed. "That would be entirely impossible, wouldn't it?"

Leah laughed. "One adopted, one the old fashioned way. It doesn't sound so impossible to me! But maybe two would completely throw off *the schedule?*"

Ben leaned toward her, his lips just inches above hers and the love in his eyes took her breath away.

"What schedule?"

Chapter Twenty-Two

The phone rang in Leah's apartment just as she finished packing another box.

"I miss you. When are you moving in?"

Just the sound of Ben's husky voice over the phone made Leah's heart lift. "When you make an honest woman of me."

Although Leah still picked up Olivia after school and spent the evenings with her and Ben, they'd decided that she should live in her apartment until their wedding day. Ben didn't want any raised eyebrows now that the word had spread about their engagement and Leah had agreed, touched that he was concerned about her reputation. If she felt lonely and disconnected, all she had to do was look at the wedding gown hanging on a hook near her bed and count the minutes to her wedding day. Which couldn't come soon enough.

"Bear misses you. He misses you so much that he

gnawed on the leg of the dining room chair you always sit in. People are going to think we have a family of beavers living in the pantry."

Leah curled up in the chair and tucked her feet underneath her. "Have him chew up the other three chairs so they match, okay?"

"Why didn't I think of that?"

Leah heard a click and Ben's sigh. "Call-waiting strikes again. Jonah is supposed to call, do you mind if I take it quick?"

"Go ahead." Leah could see her wedding dress from where she sat and just the sight of it made her smile.

"Leah?"

There was such a strange tone in Ben's voice when he came back on the line that Leah immediately tensed. "What is it?"

"I just got a phone call from a guy named Ross Van Zandt. He asked me to meet him at the Starlight."

"Who is he?" Leah tried to place the name and came up blank.

"He says he's a private investigator."

"A private..." Leah's voice trailed off as she tried to come up with a reason why a private investigator would be calling Ben for a meeting. "When?"

"In half an hour."

"Do you want me to meet you there?"

"Olivia is already asleep, could you come over and stay with her until I get back?"

Leah was already pulling on her shoes. "I'll be there in ten minutes."

"And Leah...don't forget to pray."

* * *

When Ben pulled in by the diner, he wasn't surprised to see that it was closed. After all, it was after nine o'clock at night, but what he was surprised to see was Kelly Young's car parked several spots away from his.

He could see that she was still sitting in the driver's seat, but when he got out, she jumped out and hurried toward him.

"Ben?"

Automatically, he drew her in for a quick hug. They'd been friends for years and she was almost like a sister to him. "What brings you out this time of night?"

"The same phone call you got," Kelly said. The lights from inside the diner illuminated the concern in her brown eyes.

"Ross Van Zandt called you, too?" Ben couldn't believe it. "Do you know him?"

"When he called and I hesitated about meeting him here, he mentioned that you were coming, too. Probably realized I don't know him from the latest psycho in the news and wouldn't be able to tell them apart."

"I take issue at being called a psycho," a dry voice said behind them. "Just call me Ross."

Kelly moved closer to Ben as they turned around and saw a man standing several feet away. Ben wondered how he'd managed to get so close without them realizing it.

"What's this about?" Ben said irritably, sensing Kelly's agitation. To be honest, he wasn't feeling at ease, either.

Lord, I'm not sure what's happening, but it's no surprise to You. I trust You....

"The diner is open. Why don't we sit down and have a cup of coffee?" Ross Van Zandt suggested. "I'll explain why I called you both here."

The diner, which usually was cheerfully punctuated by the sound of old 50s tunes, was eerily quiet when they walked in. Only the lights above the soda fountain were on, bathing the room in shadows.

Kelly slid into the booth next to Ben, and Ross sat across from them.

"I assume you're both aware of the falsified documents at Tiny Blessings," Ross said.

"It was in the newspaper." Ben tamped down the sudden chill that spread through him.

"We're doing everything we can to sort things out," Kelly said defensively. "If you know something, you could have called me to make an appointment."

Ross didn't seem at all fazed by her response but Ben noticed that his expression softened slightly when he looked at her. "I was hired by a woman to find the child that was stolen from her thirty-five years ago and I've narrowed it down to two possibilities. The two of you. You or Ben Cavanaugh may be the adult child of Sandra Lange."

"What!" Kelly and Ben said the word simultaneously but neither of them saw the humor in it.

Kelly's shoulders slumped forward and Ben took her hand, squeezing it reassuringly as he glared at Ross.

Ross shrugged. "I'm sorry I couldn't come up with a way to make it all warm and fuzzy for you. It's the truth. The dates coincide with the birth of her baby but circumstances surrounding the birth are cloudy. She wasn't even sure if she had a boy or a girl."

"How can that have happened?" Ben demanded.

They were so focused on Ross that neither of them noticed the woman who had silently moved to stand near the table. Until she spoke.

"I hope you can both forgive me but I just had to know. I already let too much time go by." Sandra's eyes were shadowed but she tried to smile.

Kelly's fingers tightened around Ben's and she looked away, but Ben felt a sudden hope take wing inside him. Was it possible that after all these years his birth mother had been so close? Quickly he scanned the woman's features, looking for glimpse of his own.

"Sit down, Sandra," Ross said, his voice gentle. "I'll get some coffee. We could all probably use some right about now."

Instead of sitting in the booth with them, Sandra pulled up a chair, the lines in her face so prominent that Ben momentarily forgot his own feelings. This couldn't be easy for her, either. He'd heard about her battle with cancer.

In the next half hour, Sandra haltingly explained how she'd been abandoned by her baby's father but when she'd experienced complications during labor, he'd shown up and asked her to sign some papers, which he'd told her had to do with insurance payments. Still under the affects of the anesthesia, Sandra had signed them, but when she woke up, both her baby and the father were gone. Barnaby Harcourt had falsified the records and placed the baby up for adoption.

Ben, absorbed in her story, listened in disbelief. It wasn't possible that something so underhanded could actually have happened in their hometown. He glanced at Kelly and tears were streaming down her face. She believed her. And in the space of a moment, he realized that he did, too.

"We need both of you to agree to DNA tests," Ross interjected when Sandra finished her story. She was crying, too, and for a split second Ben's eyes met Ross's, and he realized the guy felt just as helpless as he did as to what to do next. Two women who needed comfort and he was so numb that he didn't know how to offer it.

"Who is the…father?" Ben asked.

Sandra shook her head. "I can't tell you that."

"You *won't* tell us," Kelly said, finding her voice.

Sandra nodded. "It's…just trust me. Please. I can't tell you that yet."

Trust her? Ben didn't know who to trust at the moment. Not Ross Van Zandt, who'd obviously been investigating him for some time. Not even Sandra, the woman who'd hired him.

Trust me.

The two quiet words cleared his head immediately and all the emotions that were stewing inside him calmed. No matter how this turned out, he was going to stick close to God this time.

"Fine." He looked at Sandra and forced a smile. "I agree to a DNA test."

"I will, too," Kelly said softly.

There were at least a hundred more questions that

Ben wanted to have answered, but until they found out which one of them was really Sandra's child, he knew he'd have to wait.

"I'm sorry we had to do it this way," Ross said, rising to his feet and signaling an end to the meeting. "But I hit a brick wall with those falsified documents, so Sandra and I decided the best thing to do would be to tell you both the truth and ask you to agree to the test."

"So what now?" Kelly said, looking at Ross.

"I'll set it up with the hospital," he said, standing almost protectively at Sandra's side. "We'll be in touch."

All the way home, Ben could see Sandra's stricken expression. The way she wouldn't quite look them in the eye, as if she blamed herself that her baby was stolen from her in the hospital.

Leah was waiting for him in the hallway and she melted into his arms. And as tiny and slender as she was, at the moment she was his rock.

"It's bad news?" she murmured.

"It's definitely *sitting down* news," Ben said, leading her to the sofa in the living room.

Leah could tell by the expression on Ben's face that whatever Ross Van Zandt had told him at the diner had momentarily shifted his world, but nothing could have prepared her for the truth.

"Sandra Lange?" All this time, Ben's birth mother was so close?

"We'll find out within the next week or so," Ben said. "But she wouldn't tell us who the father is."

Leah, given her own past experiences, knew that Sandra had a reason for that. "I feel sorry for her. Going through the cancer treatments alone. Dealing with the things that happened to her."

Ben remembered the peace he'd seen in Sandra's eyes. Even in the midst of the tears, he'd recognized it for what it was. Somewhere along the way, Sandra Lange had given her life to the Lord. She was trusting Him to work all this out and because of Leah's influence, he knew he could do the same.

"Have I told you today that I love you?" Ben asked, stopping Leah in midsentence.

"I think you may have…once or twice. But what has that got to do with all of this?" Her eyes began to sparkle.

"You know that verse about 'a future and a hope'?" Ben murmured.

"Yes…"

"God gave me a reminder of that verse."

"What?"

Ben traced the side of her face gently with his fingers. "You."

Leah's breath caught in her throat. "Ben…"

"I am so tired of trying to arrange everything so it comes out right. Whatever happens with Sandra, I'm going to trust that God will work it out the way He wants. It's occurred to me lately that His plans are better than anything I could come up with."

Leah giggled. "Is that so?"

Ben pulled her closer. "Remember my example?"

"Me?"

Just before Ben's lips met hers, she heard his answer.

"Us."

* * * * *

Dear Reader,

It was an honor to be asked to be part of the TINY BLESSINGS continuity series and to work with such a talented group of authors. It was a challenge, but I loved every minute of it.

I hope you enjoyed getting to know Leah and Ben in *Her Christmas Wish.* Sometimes it's easy to feel like Ben did—that if we do everything "right" we'll be spared heartache or pain. It took Leah, who had truly let God's love shine through the broken places in her life, to remind him that God doesn't promise we'll have an easy life, but He does promise He'll never leave us. Our future and our hope are found in Him.

Many blessings,

Kathryn Springer

P.S.: I love to hear from my readers. You can contact me at kspringwrites@excite.com!

Sandra's missing child is revealed in
PAST SECRETS, PRESENT LOVE,
the final book in the TINY BLESSINGS *series.*
For a sneak preview, please turn the page.
And keep reading for an extra-special bonus!

"How'd you do it?"

Kelly twisted in her seat and stared at Ross. "Excuse me?"

"Your car, pasted against that tree. How'd it happen?"

"I'm not sure." She tried to re-create the sequence of events in her head. "The steering seemed wonky," she mused.

"Wonky?" Ross put on his left signal and waited for a car to pass before he turned toward the church. "What does that mean?"

"Soft, spongy. Unresponsive." What part didn't he understand?

"Has it happened before?" He frowned when she shook her head. "It's a new model, isn't it?"

Kelly nodded. "I just got it in the fall."

"Then it shouldn't be a maintenance problem. Maybe some manufacturing defect is to blame."

Remembering, she shuddered. "I'm just glad I wasn't on a freeway when it happened. As it was I missed a little boy by inches." She chided herself for forgetting her manners. "I'm glad that you were driving past. Thank you."

"No problem."

She studied his thick jacket and jeans. "You're not going to Ben and Leah's wedding?"

"Nah. I'm not all that big on church stuff." He pulled up near the door, glanced around. "Looks like you beat the bridal party to the church."

"That's a blessing. Thank you very much for coming to my rescue and for handling the tow for me, Ross." She handed over her keys, then rested her hand on the door handle, wondering if she should say it. "You know they'd love you to come. Why don't you at least attend the reception?"

"I'm waiting for a call from the lab," he told her. "About the DNA tests."

Kelly froze. She knew exactly what he was talking about. Both she and Ben had given samples for testing last week.

Don't let me be her daughter!

"I didn't realize you'd find out so soon," Kelly whispered, staring at her feet. They were bare. She used her toes to grope for her shoes.

"You mean you were hoping." His voice held a hint of condemnation.

"I have a full, rich life," she told him, bristling a little. "I loved my parents. They gave me a wonderful life. It's not that easy to suddenly accept that someone I've known for years could be my biological mother."

"Someone you feel would take away the glory from your mother, is that what you're saying?"

"I guess. Sort of." It was more complicated than that, but Kelly had deliberately avoided probing her feelings to discover what lay beneath her sense of fear about this situation.

"Sandra's not asking for anything, Kelly." He reached out, touched the hand she'd clenched on her lap. "She just wants to know the child she gave birth to all those years ago."

"So you've said." Kelly opened the door, felt the sting of the cold crisp air hit her in a wave. Impulsively she turned, faced him. "But I already had a wonderful mother whom I dearly loved," she blurted out. "Nobody can take her place."

Kelly didn't wait for the argument she knew would follow. She didn't want to hear it. Instead she swung her legs out of the car, and rose. Then she bent and met his frowning stare.

"Tell Vinnie I'll manage without the car until he gets it fixed. And thanks for the ride. I appreciate it very much." She swung the door closed and hurried toward the church door, stuffing away all the doubts that had surfaced in the last few minutes.

"Please let it be Ben," she murmured over and over as she hung up her coat, then was shown to her seat. "Please, please let Sandra's child be Ben and not me."

She sat in her pew, unable to relax until Reverend Fraser had taken his place at the front and Olivia, Ben's precocious seven-year-old daughter, began her stroll down the aisle, preceding the bride. She heard a rustle at the back and twisted in time to see Caleb and Anne sneak into a back pew. So they'd made it back from their honeymoon for the wedding! Caleb still had a week off from his duties as youth minister for the Chestnut Grove

Youth Center and she'd specifically told Anne to forget about the books at Tiny Blessings for two weeks. Kelly suspected they'd disappear as quietly as they'd arrived to finish celebrating their own nuptials.

Anne looked so happy, so content. A frisson of envy twigged at her. It must be nice to have somebody to share with, somebody to help when life got to be too much.

Kelly pushed away the longing and turned back to concentrate on the ceremony. By the time the wedding march sounded, she'd almost convinced herself that everything in her world was just the same as it had always been.

Almost.

If you liked the FAITH ON THE LINE *series
from Love Inspired, you'll love
the* FAITH AT THE CROSSROADS *series,
coming in January from Love Inspired Suspense!
And now, turn the page for a sneak preview of
A TIME TO PROTECT by Lois Richer,
the first installment of*
FAITH AT THE CROSSROADS.
*On sale in January 2006
from Steeple Hill Books.*

Brendan Montgomery switched his beeper to vibrate and slid it back inside his shirt pocket. Nothing was going to spoil Manuel DeSantis Vance's first birthday party—and this large Vance and Montgomery gathering—if he could help it.

Peter Vance's puffed out chest needed little explanation. He was as formidable as any father proudly displaying his beloved child. Peter's wife Emily waited on Manuel's other side, posing for the numerous photographs Yvette Duncan insisted posterity demanded. Apparently posterity was greedy.

Judging by the angle of her camera, Brendan had a hunch Yvette's lens sidetracked from the parents to the cake she'd made for Manuel. Who could blame her? That intricate train affair must have taken hours to create and assemble, and little Manuel obviously appreciated her efforts.

"Make sure you don't chop off their heads this time, Yvette." As the former mayor of Colorado Springs, Frank Montgomery had opinions on everything. And as Yvette's mentor, he'd never been shy about offering her his opinion, especially on all aspects of picture-taking. But since Yvette's camera happened to be the latest in digital technology and Frank had never owned one, Brendan figured most of his uncle's free advice was superfluous and probably useless. But he wouldn't be the one to tell him so.

"Don't tell me what to do, Frank," Yvette ordered adjusting the camera. "Just put your arm around your wife. Liza, can you get him to smile?" Satisfied, Yvette motioned for Dr. Robert Fletcher and his wife Pamela, who were Manuel's godparents, and their two young sons to line up behind the birthday boy.

Brendan eased his way into the living room and found a horde of Montgomery and Vance family members lounging around the room, listening to a news report on the big-screen television.

"Alistair Barclay, the British hotel mogul now infamous for his ties to a Latin American drug cartel, died today under suspicious circumstances. Currently in jail, Barclay was accused of running a branch of the notorious crime syndicate right here in Colorado Springs. The drug cartel originated in Venezuela under the direction of kingpin Baltasar Escalante, whose private plane crashed some months ago while he was attempting to escape the CIA. Residents of Colorado Springs have worked long and hard to free their city from the grip of crime—"

"Hey, guys, this is a party. Let's lighten up." Brendan reached out and pressed the mute button, followed by a chorus of groans. "You can listen to the same newscast tonight, but we don't want to spoil Manuel's big day with talk of drug cartels and death, do we?"

His brother Quinn winked and took up his cause. "Yeah, what's happened with that cake, anyway? Are we ever going to eat it? I'm starving."

"So is somebody else, apparently," Yvette said, appearing in the doorway, her flushed face wreathed in a grin. "Manuel already got his thumb onto the train track and now he's covered in black icing. His momma told him he had to wait till the mayor gets here, though, so I guess you'll just have to do the same, Quinn."

Good-natured groans filled the room.

"Maxwell Vance has been late since he got elected into office," Fiona Montgomery said, her eyes dancing with fun. "Maybe one of us should give him a call and remind him his grandson is waiting for his birthday cake. In fact, I'll do it myself."

"Leave the mayor alone, Mother. He already knows your opinion on pretty much everything," Brendan said, sharing a grin with Quinn.

"It may be that the mayor has been delayed by some important meeting." Alessandro Donato spoke up from his seat in the corner. "After Thanksgiving, that is the time when city councilors and mayors iron out their budgets, yes?"

"But just yesterday I talked to our mayor about that, in regard to a story I'm doing on city finances." Brendan's cousin Colleen sat cross-legged on the floor, her hair tied back in the eternal ponytail she favored. "He said they hadn't started yet."

Something about the way Alessandro moved when he heard Colleen's comment sent a nerve in Brendan's neck to twitching, enough to make him take a second look at the man. Moving up through the ranks of the FBI after his time as a police officer had only happened because Brendan usually paid attention to that nerve. Right now it was telling him to keep an eye on the tall, lean man named Alessandro, even if he was Lidia Vance's nephew.

There was something about Alessandro that didn't quite fit. What was the story on this guy anyway?

A phone rang. Brendan chuckled when everyone in the room checked their pockets. The grin faded when Alessandro spoke into his. His face paled, his body tensed. He murmured one word, then listened.

"Hey, something's happening! Turn up the TV, Brendan," Colleen said. Everyone was staring at the screen where a reporter stood in front of city hall.

Brendan raised the volume.

"Mayor Vance was apparently on his way to a family event when the shot was fired. Excuse me, I'm getting an update." The reporter lifted one hand to press the earpiece closer. "I'm told there may have been more than one shot fired. As I said, at this moment, Maxwell Vance is on his way to the hospital. Witnesses say he was bleeding profusely from his head and chest, though we have no confirmed details. We'll update you as the situation develops."

Love Inspired® SUSPENSE

RIVETING INSPIRATIONAL ROMANCE

Sounds *of* Silence

by Elizabeth White

THE TEXAS GATEKEEPERS

When a seven-year-old is witness to a murder, Isabel Valenzuela goes into isolation with the frightened child to try to draw information to solve the case. Working closely with U.S. Border Patrol agent Eli Carmichael, Isabel finds her faith in God tested as she becomes more involved with Eli and the crime.

"White shows the meaning of being Christian without preaching."
—*Library Journal*

Love Inspired

THE McKASLIN CLAN

BLESSED VOWS

BY

JILLIAN HART

After promising his dying brother he'd care for his little girl, tech sergeant Jake McCall needed a wife—and Rachel McKaslin was the answer to his prayers. But the love he had for his "convenient" wife didn't stem from duty. Would he survive his dangerous mission and return to confess his true feelings?

The McKaslin Clan: Ensconced in a quaint mountain town overlooking the vast Montana plains, the McKaslins rejoice in the powerful bonds of faith, family... and forever love.

Don't miss BLESSED VOWS

On sale December 2005

Available at your favorite retail outlet.

www.SteepleHill.com

REQUEST YOUR FREE BOOKS!

2 FREE INSPIRATIONAL NOVELS
PLUS A
FREE
MYSTERY GIFT

Love Inspired

YES! Please send me 2 FREE Love Inspired® novels and my FREE mystery gift. After receiving them, if I don't wish to receive any more books, I can return the shipping statement marked "cancel." If I don't cancel, I will receive 4 brand-new novels every month and be billed just $3.99 per book in the U.S. or $4.74 per book in Canada, plus 25¢ shipping and handling per book and applicable taxes, if any*. That's a savings of over 20% off the cover price! I understand that accepting the 2 free books and gift places me under no obligation to buy anything. I can always return a shipment and cancel at any time. Even if I never buy another book from Steeple Hill, the two free books and gift are mine to keep forever.

113 IDN D74R 313 IDN D74

Name	(PLEASE PRINT)	
Address		Apt.
City	State/Prov.	Zip/Postal Code

Signature (if under 18, a parent or guardian must sign)

Order online at www.LoveInspiredBooks.com

Or mail to Steeple Hill Reader Service™:

IN U.S.A.	IN CANADA
3010 Walden Ave.	P.O. Box 609
P.O. Box 1867	Fort Erie, Ontario
Buffalo, NY 14240-1867	L2A 5X3

Not valid to current Love Inspired subscribers.

Want to try two free books from another series?
Call 1-800-873-8635 or visit www.morefreebooks.com

* Terms and prices subject to change without notice. NY residents add applicable sales tax. Canadian residents will be charged applicable provincial taxes and GST. This offer limited to one order per household. All orders subject to approval. Credit or debit balances in a customer's account(s) may be offset by any other outstanding balance owed by or to the customer.

LIRE

TITLES AVAILABLE NEXT MONTH

Don't miss these four stories in December

BLESSED VOWS by Jillian Hart
The McKaslin Clan

Jake McCall's sudden proposal surprised Rachel McKaslin—they hadn't been dating that long. The handsome military man had promised to care for his orphaned niece but was being deployed unexpectedly. Rachel's love for the child made marrying her the perfect solution. Would time apart make Jake see the true treasure he left behind?

PAST SECRETS, PRESENT LOVE by Lois Richer
Tiny Blessings

Private investigator Ross Van Zandt delivered some shocking news to Kelly Young. Now, as the director of the Tiny Blessings adoption agency tries to come to terms with the revelation, she finds herself falling for the handsome sleuth. But Ross is keeping a secret that could tear them apart....

SUGAR PLUMS FOR DRY CREEK by Janet Tronstad
When the residents of Dry Creek heard newcomer Lizette Baker name, they expected a bakery from the young businesswoman, not a dance studio. Lizette hoped her Christmas production of *The Nutcracker* would win them over, yet when she met her students' handsome guardian, her visions of sugar plums began to turn into dreams of love....

A PERFECT LOVE by Lenora Worth
Texas Hearts

Hoping a trip would help her recharge, world-weary city girl Summer Maxwell returned to her small hometown. When her car broke down on the way, landscaper Mack Riley came to her rescue, and sparks flew. Yet Summer's unresolved family problems and Mack's troubled past could put the brakes on their connection.

LICNM110